BABY BE-BOP

Also by Francesca Lia Block

FRANCESCA LIA BLOCK

BABY BE-BOP

Joanna Cotler Books

An Imprint of HarperCollins*Publishers*

Baby Be-Bop
Copyright © 1995 by Francesca Lia Block

Library of Congress Cataloging-in-Publication Data
Block, Francesca Lia.
  Baby be-bop / Francesca Lia Block.
     p.   cm.
  "Joanna Cotler books."
  Summary: Dirk McDonald, a sixteen-year-old boy living in Los Angeles, comes to
terms with being gay after he receives surreal storytelling visitations.
  ISBN 0-06-024879-3. — ISBN 0-06-024880-7 (lib. bdg.)
  [1. Homosexuality—Fiction.   2. Ghosts—Fiction.   3. Los Angeles (Calif.)—
Fiction.]   I. Title.
PZ7.B61945ab   1995   94-44314
[Fic]—dc20   CIP
                                                                   AC

Typography by Steven M. Scott
4   5   6   7   8   9   10
❖

Thank you

Irving Block
Gilda Block
Gregg Marx
Fred Drake
Julie Fallowfield
Louise Quayle
Joanna Cotler
Lillian Peel
Geoffrey Grisham
Fred Burke
Autumn Kimble
and Teddy Quinn

Part I

Dirk and Fifi

irk had known it since he could remember.

At nap time he lay on the mat, feeling his skin sticking to brown plastic, listening to the buzz of flies, smelling the honeysuckle through the faraway window, tasting the coating of graham cracker cookies and milk in his mouth, wanting to be racing through space. He tried to think of something he liked.

He was on a train with the fathers—all naked and cookie-colored and laughing. There under the blasts of warm water spurting from the walls as the train moved slick through the land. All the bunching calf muscles dripping water and biceps full of power comforted Dirk. He tried to see his own father's face but there was always too much steam.

Dirk knew that there was something about this train that wasn't right. One day he heard his Grandma Fifi talking to her canaries, Pirouette and Minuet, in the teacup-colored kitchen with honey sun pouring through the windows.

"I'm afraid it's hard for him without a man around, Pet," Fifi said as she put birdseed into the green dome-shaped cage.

The canaries chirped at her.

"I asked him about what the men and ladies on his toy train were doing, Mini, and do you know what he said? He said they were all men taking showers together."

The canaries nuzzled each other on their perch. Pet did a perfect pirouette and Mini sang.

"I guess you're right. It's something all little boys go through. It's just a phase," Fifi said.

Just a phase. Dirk thought about those words over and over again. Just a phase. Until the train inside of him would crash. Until the thing inside of him that was wrong and bad would change. Until he would change. He waited and waited for the phase to end. When would it end? He tried to do everything fast so it would end faster. He got A's in school. He ran fast. He made his body strong so that he would be picked first for teams.

That was important—being picked first. The weak, skinny, scared boys got picked last. They got chased through the yard and had their jeans pulled up hard. Sometimes other kids threw food at them. Sometimes they

4

went home with black eyes, bloody noses or swollen lips. Dirk knew that almost all the boys who were treated this way really did like girls. It was just that girls didn't like them yet. Dirk also knew that some of the boys that hurt them were doing it so they wouldn't have to think about liking boys themselves. They were burning, twisting and beating the part of themselves that might have once dreamed of trains and fathers.

Dirk knew that the main thing was to keep to himself and never to seem afraid.

Every Saturday afternoon his Grandma Fifi took him to see a matinee, where he could hide, dreaming, in crackling popcorn darkness. They saw James Dean in *Rebel Without a Cause*. That was who he wanted to be. He practiced squinting and pouting. He turned up his jacket collar and rolled his jeans. He slicked back his hair, carefully leaving one stray piece falling into his eyes. James Dean was beautiful because he didn't seem afraid of anything, but when Dirk looked into his eyes he knew that he secretly was and it made Dirk love him even more.

Grandma Fifi had two friends named Martin and Merlin who were afraid in a way Dirk didn't want to be. They were both very handsome and kind and always brought candies and toys when they came over for tea and Fifi's famous pastries. But as much as Dirk liked Martin and Merlin he knew he was different from them. They talked in voices as pale and soft as the shirts they wore and they moved as gracefully as Fifi did. Their eyes were startled and sad. They had been hurt because of who they were. Dirk didn't want to be hurt that way. He wanted to be strong and to love someone who was strong; he wanted to meet any gaze, to laugh under the brightest sunlight and never hide.

Dirk especially didn't want to hide from Grandma Fifi but he wasn't sure how to tell her. He didn't want to disturb the world she had made for him in her cottage with the steep chocolate frosting roof, the birdbath held by a nymph and the seven stone dwarfs in the garden. There were so many butterflies in that garden that when Dirk was a little boy he could stand naked in a crowd of them and be completely covered. Jade-green pupas hung from the bushes like earrings. Fifi showed Dirk the gold sparks that would later become the butterflies' orange color. Then the pupa darkened and stretched and finally a fragile monarch bloomed. Fifi and Dirk put flower nectar or a mixture of honey and water on their fingertips and the newborn butterflies crawled onto them, all ticklish, and practiced fanning wings that were like amber stained glass in the sun. In the garden there were also little butterflies that looked like petals blown from the roses with the almond scent. There were peaches with pits that also smelled and looked like almonds when you cracked them open. Fifi showed Dirk how to pinch the honeysuckle blossoms that grew over the back gate so that sweet drops fell onto his tongue. She showed him how to pinch the snapdragons' jaws to make them sing. If Dirk ever cut himself playing, Fifi broke off a piece of the thick green aloe vera plant she called Love and a gel oozed out like Love's clear, thick blood. Fifi put the gel onto Dirk's cut and stuck a Peanuts Band-Aid over it; the cut always healed by the next day, skin smooth as if it had never been broken.

Fifi had a cat named Kit who had arrived through the window one evening while an Edith Piaf record was playing and never left. Kit had pinkish fur like the tints Fifi put in her white hair. If Dirk or Fifi ever had an ache or a pain, Kit would come and sit on the part of the body that hurt them—just sit and purr. She was very warm, and after a while the soreness would disappear.

"Kit is a great healer in a cat's body," Fifi said.

Kaboodle the Noodle was Fifi's dog. He had a valentine nose, long Greta Garbo lashes and a tiny shock of hair that stood straight up. When you were sad he kissed your hand and winked at you.

Dirk and Fifi and Kaboodle went shopping at the fruit stands on Fairfax that were covered with pink netting to keep out the flies. Kaboodle sat out in front and waited.

Fifi bought bags of asparagus and bananas, kiwis and radishes, persimmons and yams. There was a little Middle Eastern market where she bought bottles of rose water and coffee beans as dark as chocolate. Fifi made pastries shaped like shells, ballet slippers and moons, and salads full of vegetables cut into the shapes of flowers.

Dirk knew that Fifi wanted great-grandchildren someday. She wanted to make pastries for them and teach them about how peach pits smelled like almonds, about butterflies that looked like flowers and about talking snapdragons. He knew he was her only chance. Worst of all, he knew she wanted him to be happy and how could he be happy in this world, he wondered, if what he knew about himself was true? So Dirk didn't tell Fifi. He didn't tell anyone. He kept to himself. He waited for the phase to end. Until the day he met Pup Lambert.

Dirk and Pup

The air smelled like lemon Pledge, sweet jasmine and mock orange. Bougainvillea grew thick up the fences like walls of paper flowers. Morning glories glowed neon purple, twining among the pink oleander. Nasturtiums shimmered along the ground like fallen sunlight.

As Dirk walked home from school he heard a whistle, and he looked up into an olive tree. In the branches sat a boy. He had brown hair with leaves in it, freckles on his turned-up nose and a Cheshire cat grin.

"Hey," the boy said.

"Hey," said Dirk.

"Want to shoot some baskets?" the boy asked.

"Sure."

The boy jumped out of the tree, landing lightly on the white rubber soles of his baby-blue Vans deck shoes.

Dirk and the boy shot baskets in the driveway of the

pale yellow house with the pink camellias growing in front. Dirk was taller, but the boy was light on his feet and had perfect aim. Dirk's heart was beating fast like the basketball hitting the pavement again and again; he was sweating.

When a car pulled into the driveway the boy grabbed the basketball and took off down the street.

"Come on," he shouted.

Dirk stood still, looking at the boy and then into the car. A heavyset man got out. Dirk just had time to wonder how such a big man could have such a quick and slender son when the man said, "Scram! I told you not to hang around here anymore! I'll call the cops!"

Dirk ran after the boy. When he caught up with him, at the edge of a field of wildflowers, he was out of breath. The sweat was getting into his eyes.

"I thought that was your house," Dirk said.

The boy grinned. "Nope."

They stood under the shifting sunlight, laughing. Dirk thought their laughter would look like sunlight through leaves if he could see it. A flock of poppies, with their faces toward the sun, moved in the breeze as if they were laughing too. Dirk noticed that the boy's ears came to slight points at the top.

"I'm Pup," the boy said.

"Dirk."

"Hey, Dirk. Next time we'll borrow someone's swimming pool."

Two days later Pup jumped out of the tree again. He and Dirk climbed the fence of an ivy-covered Spanish house with a terra-cotta roof, and stripped down to their underwear. Then they took turns diving into the aqua water. Pup did more and more elaborate dives—cannonballs and flips and flailing-in-the-air things—and Dirk tried to imitate him. They stayed in the pool until the tips of their fingers looked crinkled and crushed, and then they dried out on the hot cement. Pup had freckles on his shoulders and a gold dusting of hair on his arms and legs. With his wet hair slicked back Dirk thought he looked like James Dean.

"Are you hungry?" Dirk asked Pup.

"Starving."

Dirk and Pup went to Farmer's Market where the air smelled like tropical fruit, chilled flowers, Cajun corn bread, Belgian waffles, deli meats and cheeses, coffee and the gooey sheets of saltwater taffy that spun round and round behind glass. The light filtered softly through the striped circus tent awnings. Wind chimes and coffee cups sang. Dirk looked for Pup but couldn't find him. Then he heard a whistle. He followed the sound to a corner table where Pup was sitting behind a huge banana cream pie. He handed Dirk a fork.

"Want some?"

"Where'd you get that?" Dirk asked.

Pup grinned his Cheshire grin.

Nothing had ever tasted so good to Dirk as that frothy concoction—peaks of meringue and melts of banana—that Pup had lifted so slyly from the pie counter. But the next day Dirk asked Grandma Fifi to make a pie so Pup wouldn't have to steal and invited his friend over for dinner.

After school they went to Fifi's cottage through the backyards of houses, leaping fences and climbing walls, patting dogs and dodging the lemons that one woman threw at them. Pup gathered avocados, roses and sprigs of cherry blossoms as he ran so that by the time he met Grandma Fifi at the front door he had almost more presents than he could carry.

"This is Pup," Dirk told her.

"Pleased to meet you, Pup," said Grandma Fifi. "Thank you for the alligator pears and the flowers."

"This is my Grandma Fifi," Dirk said.

"Hi," said Pup. He seemed suddenly shy. He shook the tips of his hair out of his eyes. He lowered his eyelashes.

"Come in for some snacks," said Fifi.

She brought out guava cream cheese pastries and a pitcher of lemonade. Pup gulped and swallowed as if he hadn't had food in days.

Then Dirk showed Pup the comics that he drew. They were about two boys who turned into the superheroes

Slam and Jam when there was danger.

"You're serious," Pup said.

They lay on the floor of Dirk's room reading comics until the room turned jacaranda-blossom-purple with evening and the glow-in-the-dark constellations that Fifi had pasted on the ceiling began to come out.

"Superheroes aren't afraid of anything," Pup said softly, his voice fading with the light.

Kit jumped off the windowsill where she had been gazing at the blur of a hummingbird in the bottlebrush bush and sat on Pup's chest, over his heart. Kaboodle licked between his fingers.

"You don't seem afraid of much," said Dirk.

"I'm afraid of everything. That's why I do stuff. My mom is afraid of everything too but she just stays inside. She's afraid to go to the market, even."

"You can come over and eat with us when you want," Dirk said. "My grandma would like it."

"Thanks," said Pup.

He stayed for chicken pot pie with carrots and peas and peach pie for dessert. When you asked Fifi for pie you got it.

While they ate their dessert Fifi played an old record.

"Chills run up and down my spine / Aladdin's lamp is mine," the singer crooned, and Dirk felt silvery chills, saw, beneath his eyelids, the glinting lamp of love.

13

"This is cool music," Pup said.

"Do you dance, Pup?" Fifi asked.

"Not really," Pup said. "But I'm willing to have some lessons."

Fifi blushed. "Oh, I'm not very good anymore."

"That's not true," Dirk said. "She's a cool dancer."

"Show me," Pup said.

He stood and offered Fifi his hand. She took it, putting his other arm around her waist. Dirk watched as Fifi led Pup around the room so skillfully that it appeared he was leading her. But that was also because Pup was a natural dancer. Dirk watched how he held his head, proud on his straight strong neck, the way his shoulders curved.

"Your turn now, Dirk," Fifi said.

Dirk wasn't embarrassed the way he would have been around anyone else except Pup. Fifi felt light in his arms as they danced over the garlands of roses on the carpet. Pirouette and Mini did a waltz in their cage. Kaboodle sat up on his hind legs and offered Pup his paws. While Pup danced with Kaboodle, Kit watched them all from the mantelpiece.

When the record ended Pup insisted on skateboarding home although Fifi tried to offer him a ride. He and Dirk planned to meet in the quad at school the next day at lunch.

That morning Dirk told Fifi he was especially hungry

so when he opened his lunch there was one sandwich with cheese, avocado, lettuce, pickles, artichoke hearts, olives, red onion and mustard and one with peanut butter, raspberry jam, honey, bananas and strawberries, both on home-baked bread.

"She always does that," Dirk said, pulling out the sandwiches and shaking his head. "Would you eat one of these, Pup?"

"Are you sure?"

"She acts all hurt when I bring one home but she keeps giving them to me."

Every day after that Fifi put two sandwiches in Dirk's lunch. She never asked her grandson why he had started to eat twice the normal amount. She just beamed at him and said, "You are growing so tall and strong. And so is your friend Pup Lambert. When I first met him I was sad to see how thin he was."

"I love you, Fifi," said Dirk.

"I love you, Dirk," Fifi said.

After school Pup and Dirk listened to music in Dirk's room. They could play it loud because Fifi was a bit hard of hearing. On the wall was a chalk drawing Dirk had made of Jimi Hendrix.

"That is hell of cool," said Pup. "You are a phenomenal artist, man."

Dirk tried to concentrate on keeping his ears from turning red.

"My mom went out with this gross trucker guy once," Pup told him. "He saw the Jimi poster in my room and goes, 'That nigger looks like he's got a mouth full of cum.' I wanted to kill him. I told my mom I would if she didn't stop seeing him."

"Did she?"

"Yeah. But I don't think that's why. Her next boyfriend saw my Bowie poster and started calling him a fag. My mom said if I ever dressed like that she'd kick me out of the house."

Dirk and Pup looked up at Jimi burning his guitar. It flamed beneath the steeple of his hands, between his legs. Jimi had said it was like a sacrifice. He loved his guitar. He was giving up something he loved. Dirk wondered if Jimi had felt that way about life.

"We should start a band," Dirk said.

"Can you play?" asked Pup.

"A little. I mess around with my dad's guitar."

Dirk got out the guitar that he kept hidden in the closet.

Pup stroked it. Dirk had never seen him touch anything with such concentrated love except for Kit and Kaboodle. Just like Kit and Kaboodle, the guitar seemed to love Pup. Dirk imagined he could hear it singing in Pup's arms although Pup's fingers never touched the strings.

16

"It's beautiful," Pup said. "Your dad was cool."

"I don't remember him," Dirk said.

"What happened?"

"My mom and dad died in a crash."

Pup looked up at the picture Dirk had drawn of his hero standing with his hands in his jeans pockets, shoulders hunched, feet rolling out.

"Like James Dean?"

"Kind of."

Pup's eyes got big. "I bet your dad looked like James Dean," he said. " 'Cause you do."

Dirk picked up the guitar and bent to tune it so that Pup wouldn't see that his ears were turning red. He felt almost as if Pup had put his arm around him and said, "I'm so sorry about your parents, Dirk. I wish they were alive."

Pup took a cigarette out of his pocket.

"Where did you get that?" Dirk asked.

"I steal them from my mom."

He lit the cigarette and handed it to Dirk. Dirk hesitated. He didn't want Pup to see him cough like someone who had never smoked before.

"You know I still cough sometimes," Pup said as if he could read Dirk's mind. "And I've been smoking for a year."

Dirk inhaled. He could feel where Pup's lips had been, moist on the paper end. Pup was unscrewing one of

17

the large brass balls on Dirk's bedposts. "This is perfect," he said.

"For what?" Dirk coughed.

"For a tobacco stash," said Pup, depositing another cigarette inside the ball.

After he met Pup, Dirk's room became full of secrets. The cigarettes in the bedposts. The stolen Three Musketeers bars in the dresser drawer. The *Playboy* magazines under the bed. And the real secret that had always been there grew larger and larger each day until Dirk thought it would burst out licking its lips and rolling its eyeballs and telling everyone that Dirk McDonald wasn't normal.

Dirk looked at the *Playboy*s that Pup brought, trying to feel something. All he could think of was that the giant breasts must keep the women safe somehow, protected. As if the breasts were padding for their hearts. His own was so close to the surface of his chest. He was afraid Pup might be able to see it beating there.

Dirk's heart sent sparks and flares through his veins like a fast wheel on cement when he was with Pup. They rode their bikes and skateboards, popping wheelies, doing jumps and flips. Dirk wanted to do wilder and wilder things. It wasn't so much that he was competing with Pup or showing off for him; he wanted to give the tricks to Pup like offerings. He wanted to say, neither of us has to be afraid of anything anymore. Their knees and elbows were always speckled with blood and gritty dirt from falling but Fifi treated them with gel from Love's leaves.

Every morning Pup came by on his skateboard or his bike. He never let Dirk meet him at his house. Dirk wondered what Pup's room was like, what his mother was like.

"You wouldn't want to know," Pup said. "She's just all sad and scared."

Dirk didn't push Pup. It didn't matter anyway where Pup came from as long as they were together. At school they met for lunch. Dirk always had two sandwiches—sometimes he even had peanut butter and jam on waffles, which was Pup's favorite. Dirk rolled his eyes and acted as if Fifi had always given him two sandwiches. He and Pup didn't talk much at school, just sat eating and scowling into the sun. Sometimes girls walked by giggling in their pastel T-shirts, matching tight jeans and pale suede platform Corkees sandals. Pup winked at them, and they tossed their winged hair, smacked their lip-glossed lips. Dirk was glad the girls were too shy to do much more than that. Even the tough boys never approached Dirk and Pup although Dirk was always braced for it, a tension in his shoulders that never went away. It seemed Pup was braced too. His muscles were a man's already, as if his fear had formed them that way to make up for his small size. So the tough boys never bothered them. Together they were invincible. You couldn't find anything nasty to say. They were brown all year long, lean and strong, good at sports, smart; they smoked cigarettes and skateboarded. They wore Vans and their Levi's were always ripped at the knees. The most popular girls dreamed about them.

They shot baskets in strangers' driveways and swam in neighbors' pools and picked flowers and fruits from gardens for Fifi. Sometimes they borrowed dogs from backyards and took them on walks for a while, bringing them home before their owners returned.

It was not just Kaboodle—Pup loved all dogs and all dogs loved Pup. They came running up to him with worshipping eyes and licked his fingers, immediately flopping onto their backs like hot dogs to let him pet their bellies. He always had scraps of bread in his pockets for them.

"What do you think dogs dream about?" Pup asked Dirk one day as Kaboodle lay stretched on top of his Vans, long eyelashes curling as if he had styled them that way.

"I've never really thought about it."

"I think dogs dream about wind and light and leaves and squirrels and birds and when they cry they are dreaming about wolves and freeways. I wish I dreamed about those things."

20

"What do you dream about?"

"I don't know," Pup said.

Dirk was glad that Pup didn't ask him what he dreamed.

Dirk dreamed about Pup.

He dreamed they were the superheroes Slam and Jam—skateboarding in the sky over the city, rescuing hurt children and animals. The clouds were the shape and color of giant flowers. In Dirk's dream, he and Pup held each other in the center of a purple orchid cloud.

In the summer Dirk and Pup took the bus to the beach with Pup's two surfboards. Dirk never asked where he had gotten the boards but he thought Pup might have stolen them on one of his runs through the neighbors' backyards. As they waxed the boards with Mr. Zogg's Sex Wax to make them glide through the water, Pup told Dirk that surfing wasn't much different from skateboarding.

"You'll be a pro." He looked out at the horizon, measuring the swells.

Dirk followed Pup into the water with the board under his arm. All around him the ocean was blindingly bright, the color of water on a map. Through the sparkles of wet light Dirk saw Pup's smile before Pup paddled out on the surfboard, climbed onto it and was carried away like a part of the wave. Thinking about giving Pup his surfing like an embrace, Dirk plunged into the water with the board, steadying his body as the waves filled and fell beneath and around him.

Afterward they raced up the hot sand and collapsed belly-first onto their towels. They lay there until their hair was dry and the sun and salt water made their skin feel taut against their bones. Then they used the outdoor showers, peeling their trunks away from their bodies, feeling the granules of scratchy sand rinse off from between their legs in the cold water. Pup wrapped his towel around his waist and pulled off his trunks from underneath. Dirk tried not to look. He wrapped his towel the same way and tried to get out of his trunks as smoothly as possible while Pup pulled up his jeans under the towel.

Sometimes after they'd been surfing they sat at Figtree's Cafe on the Venice boardwalk drinking smoothies, eating blueberry muffins and watching the parade. There were velvet and tie-dye women who read tarot cards. Dirk never even wanted them to look at him, afraid they would guess his secret. There were kids break dancing and bulky bronze bodybuilders, a carnival of half-naked roller women, bicycle magician trickster boys, a clown who painted faces, a mocha-colored, electric blue-eyed man in a white turban who played electric guitar and warbled electric songs like a skating genie. There was an accordion-playing devil with a circus cart drawn by mangy stuffed animals on bicycles. More animals dangled from a miniature carousel, and there was a real stuffed taxidermy dog, rigid and nightmarish.

Sometimes, to get away from all of it—especially that dog carcass—Dirk and Pup walked under the arcade of pastel Corinthian columns decaying in the salt air, past the vine-covered wood-frame houses and rose-jasmine gardens on the canals and the ducks flapping their feet through the streets like little surfers.

One day after they'd been surfing Dirk started to get on the bus but Pup put his sun-warmed hand on Dirk's surf-sore biceps.

"I know a faster way."

Pup stuck out his thumb. With the freckles on his nose and his bare feet he reminded Dirk of Huckleberry Finn, his Huckleberry friend. Fifi had told Dirk never to hitchhike but Dirk didn't want to be afraid of anything, and besides Pup looked so cute standing there with his thumb out, so defiant and twinkly holding his surfboard, one hip a little higher than the other, behind him the sky turning as pink as the skin on his shoulders where his tan was peeling.

Two girls in a white convertible Mustang stopped. Dirk recognized them—it was Tracey Stace and Nancy Nance, two of the most popular girls from their school.

"Don't you know it's dangerous to pick up hitchhikers?" Pup teased.

"You guys aren't dangerous. You're too cute," Tracey Stace said. "Besides, you go to Fairfax."

She had dimples and her hair was almost white in the

sun, her breasts straining her crocheted bikini top. She was wearing cutoffs ripped the whole way up the sides to show her sleek tan thighs. Nancy Nance was a smaller, less dimpled, less cleavaged version of Tracey Stace. She flopped over into the backseat, and Dirk sat next to her. Pup sat in front with Tracey Stace.

"Want to come over?" she asked. "My mom's out of town."

Tracey Stace lived in a modern house in the hills, all wood and glass. There was a Jacuzzi in the backyard. She told Pup and Dirk to test the water while she and Nancy got what she called "refreshments." Pup slipped in. Dirk followed him, feeling big and awkward. The blasts of hot water massaged deep into the muscles of his lower back. Tracey and Nancy came out in their bikinis, carrying cold beers and a joint. Their bodies hardly made a ripple as they slid into the Jacuzzi. The moon was full, reflecting the whole of the sun. Lit up with it, the flowers in the garden looked like aliens with glowing skins. The palm trees shook in the Santa Ana winds like the hips of Hawaiian hula girls. Dirk thought about how Fifi called them palmistrees. She said she wondered if you could read their fortunes from above in the sky. He was glad that no one here could read his fortune.

Dirk watched how Pup held the joint and sucked in, narrowing his eyes. He did it too. The smoke burned

24

sweetly in his throat and chest, releasing the place in his shoulders that was always tight, ready to react, to fight back, if someone found out his secret.

Tracey smacked some pink bubblegum-scented gloss from a fat stick onto her lips and moved closer to Pup. Then Dirk watched Pup lean over, just like that, not even thinking, not even trying, and kiss Tracey Stace's mouth. Seeing Pup like that, kissing the most beautiful girl in school, made Dirk want to weep—not just because it was Tracey Stace and not Dirk who Pup was kissing but because of the beauty of it, the way Pup's hand looked against Tracey Stace's back and the way his eyes closed, the long lashes clumping together, the moonlight washing over everything like the waves that Dirk still felt pulling his body and seething beneath him although they were now miles and hours away.

Dirk turned to Nancy Nance, who looked very delicate, like a little girl. He was afraid he might crush her. Her lashes were like flickers of moonlight on her cheek.

"You're so pretty," Dirk said. He wanted her to know that if something went wrong it wasn't because of that. She smiled shyly at him and he reached out for her, eyes closed, pressing his lips against hers.

Nancy did all the work after that. Dirk's beauty was all he had to give her although he would have given her more if he could. When he felt as if she would guess his secret he looked over at Pup and Tracey Stace. Pup had his legs around her and their bodies were moving up and down in the water.

Then Pup looked at Dirk. When Dirk saw what was in Pup's eyes his heart contracted with tiny pulses, the way Nancy Nance's body was trembling near his. Dirk knew then that Pup loved him too. But mixed with Pup's love was fear and soon it was just fear sucking the love away. Pup closed his eyes and there wasn't even fear anymore. There was just a beautiful boy with pointed ears kissing a girl in a Jacuzzi, a boy who hardly knew that Dirk existed.

After what had happened with Tracey Stace and Nancy Nance, Dirk knew that everything had changed. Before Dirk and Pup had kissed the girls they were still safe in their innocence, little Peter Pans never growing old, never having to explain. Now Dirk's love for Pup raged through him bitterly. It burned his shoulders like the sun, blistering as if it could peel off layers of skin. It stung like shards of glass embedded in a wound. It jolted him awake like an electric shock.

Tracey Stace and Nancy Nance picked Pup and Dirk up at Fifi's cottage. The girls were wearing tight white jeans that laced up front and back and lace-up T-shirts.

"Where we going?" Pup asked, kissing Tracey Stace's cheek.

"A dance club in the valley," Tracey said.

"We don't dance," Pup said. "We hate disco."

"It's not a disco place. They play KROQ music."

"We still don't dance," said Pup.

Dirk was glad he hadn't told them about dancing with Fifi in the kitchen.

"You can watch us," Tracey said and Nancy giggled.

Dirk and Pup sat behind the dj booth watching Tracey's and Nancy's blond hair change colors under the strobe lights as they danced to Adam and the Ants, Devo, and the Go-Gos. Pup lit up a cigarette. Dirk waited for Pup to hand it to him but instead Pup held out the pack. Dirk took his own cigarette. It was the first time they hadn't shared.

"I scored a whole pack this time," Pup said, as if he were explaining it.

Dirk looked at Pup, far away behind a cloud of blue smoke, moving farther and farther away. Tracey and Nancy were twisting, snaking, shaking and skanking all over the floor. When "Los Angeles" by X came on they butted heads and collided into each other, working their elbows and knees in all directions.

"Punk rock," Tracey shrilled.

Punk rock, Dirk thought as a boy jumped off the carpeted bench along the mirrored wall and began slamming with invisible demons. With his stiff sunglass-black Mohawk, rows of earrings and black leather boots, the sweat and strength of his body, he made Tracey and Nancy's imitation look like hopscotch.

Dirk could almost feel Pup's heart slamming inside of him as he watched the boy. Dirk knew, seeing that dancer, alone and proud, tormented and beautiful, that he had found something he wanted to be. The boy reminded Dirk of Wild Animal Park.

When he was little Fifi had taken him on the wild animal safari. You had to keep the windows rolled up so the animals couldn't get in. Dirk wanted to get out of the car and run around with them. They were fierce and wise and easy in their skins. That was what the dancing boy reminded Dirk of.

"That dude has some hell of cool boots," Pup said, flicking ashes.

Tracey and Nancy danced over. "She told you this wasn't a disco," Nancy said.

"I think punk is gross," said Tracey.

When they left the club that night Dirk saw Mohawk and three other boys with short hair and black clothes leaning against a turquoise-blue-and-white '55 Pontiac in the parking lot, smoking.

"My grandmother drives a car like that," Dirk said. "A red-and-white one."

He looked back at the boys as Tracey Stace drove away.

"Want to come over?" Tracey asked.

"I'm feeling kind of burnt," Dirk said. "You can just drop me off."

Pup didn't come by Dirk's house the next day. Dirk felt like his stomach was a roller coaster as he rode his skateboard to school. At lunchtime he looked for Pup. He was sitting with Tracey Stace and Nancy Nance.

"What's up?" Dirk asked.

"Not much," Pup said. "You should have hung with us last night. We drove up to Mulholland."

"Where were you this morning?" Dirk asked.

He saw Pup's upper lip curl slightly. "Tracey gave me a ride. We were out all night."

For three days Pup didn't come by Dirk's house. When Dirk finally called and asked him what he was doing that night Pup said, "I'm seeing Tracey." That was all. He didn't ask Dirk to join them.

Dirk saw Pup and Tracey walking on campus with their hands in the back pockets of each other's jeans and knew that he had to do something. If he didn't tell Pup his feelings he thought he might go slamming through space, careening into everything until there was nothing left of him but bruises wilting on bone. He caught up with Pup in the hall after school.

"Are you free today, man?" Dirk asked.

Pup looked like a startled animal caught in the beam of headlights in the middle of a road.

"I'm seeing Tracey," he said. It didn't sound mean, just sad, Dirk thought.

"Just meet me at the tree this afternoon." Dirk walked away.

He didn't really expect Pup to be at the tree where they had first met. It was a warm day but he kept his Wayfarer sunglasses on, kept his sweatshirt on. He practiced skateboard tricks on the sidewalk under the olive tree where Pup and he had put their footprints once when the cement was wet. He was skateboarding over the black stains of smashed olives and the footprints when he heard the thud of rubber Vans soles on cement, and there was Pup with leaves in his hair just like the first day.

"Hey," Pup said.

"Hey," said Dirk, flipping his skateboard into the air and catching it. He gestured with his head and started walking. Pup walked much more slowly than usual. Dirk could smell his scent—clean like salt water and honeysuckle and grass.

"Want to stop by the house?" Dirk asked.

Pup shrugged. They were silent the whole way to the cottage.

Jimi Hendrix on the stereo. Pup slouched on the floor in Dirk's room while Dirk unscrewed the bedpost and took out what he had hidden there. He shook the pot into the paper and rolled and licked the way the boy who had sold it to him had done. Then he lit the joint and handed it to Pup. Pup took a deep hit and handed it back. Dirk breathed in smoke like the green and golden afternoon light. Maybe it would make him brave.

"Nancy really likes you," Pup said after his second hit. "She's a babe."

"She is," said Dirk.

"You should've gone with us up to Mulholland."

Dirk wanted a magical plant to grow inside of him, making him proud and at ease. He and Pup smoked some more. Jimi's guitar burned with music.

"I just wanted to tell you. I've been pretending my whole life. I'm so sick of it. You're my best friend." Dirk looked down, feeling the heat in his face.

"Don't even say it, Dirk," said Pup.

Dirk started to reach out his hand but drew it back. He started to open his mouth to explain but Pup whispered, "Please don't. I can't handle it, man."

He got up and pushed his hair out of his eyes. "I love you, Dirk," Pup said. "But I can't handle it."

And then before Dirk knew it, Pup was gone.

That night Dirk stood in the bathroom looking at his reflection. He didn't see the fine angles of his cheekbones, the delicate bridge of his nose, the tenderness of his lips. He didn't see the sparkle of his dark eyes that seemed to shine up from the deepest, brightest place. He saw a scared boy who was in love with Pup Lambert and who hated himself.

Dirk took a razor and began to shave the sides of his scalp. The buzz vibrated into his brain. How thin was the skin at his temples, Dirk thought. Just skin stretched over pulse. He thought about the punk rock boy at the dance club. There was something about that boy that no one could touch. Dirk took the hair that was left on his head and dyed it with black dye so that it was almost blue. Then he formed it into a spikey fan. He smoothed it with Fifi's gel and sprayed it with her Aqua Net so it stood straight up like the hair on top of Kaboodle's head.

At school Dirk wore all black and his Mohawk. Everyone turned and stared. But no one had questions in their eyes about what it was all hiding underneath. The disguise worked. There was some fear, some admiration, some jealousy, but no one despised Dirk the way he knew they would if he revealed his secret.

Also, no one questioned why Dirk and Pup didn't share a lunch on the same bench anymore, why they didn't play basketball together. It all seemed because of the Mohawk, the big boots Dirk had started to wear, the Germs and X buttons on his collar. That seemed like enough. No one knew that it was because of a glance in a Jacuzzi, a joint shared like a kiss and then turned to ash, a shock of love.

Dirk and the Tear Jerks

ifi watched Dirk and his Mohawk more closely now. Her blue eyes looked always ready to spill. Dirk wanted to tell her, how he wanted to tell her, but what if the tears spilled, blue onto her cheeks? What if he hurt the one person who had loved him his whole life? What if she said, "It's just a phase," and he had to tell her, "It's not just a phase, Grandma Fifi. It's who I am."

And why did he have to tell? Boys who loved girls didn't have to sit their mothers down and say, "Mom, I love girls. I want to sleep with them." It would be too embarrassing. Just because what he felt was different, did it have to be discussed?

On Dirk's sixteenth birthday Fifi called him into the kitchen.

"Where's Pup?" Fifi asked. "I thought you were going to invite him over."

"He's busy," Dirk said. "You know that. You ask me every day."

Kit came and sat on Dirk's lap. Kaboodle covered his eyes with his paws. Pet and Mini did a tragic ballet in their cage.

Fifi had baked Dirk a chocolate raspberry kiwi cake. The candles made her shine like the Christmas tree angel she put on her pink-flocked tree each year. Dirk closed his eyes and blew the candles out. He didn't make a wish. There were no wishes inside of him anymore.

"I have something for you, sweetie," Fifi said.

Kaboodle winked at him and licked frosting off his fingers.

Dirk followed Fifi outside, Kaboodle bouncing at their feet so that his tongue swung with each step. Fifi's red-and-white 1955 Pontiac convertible was parked in the driveway. It had a huge red ribbon tied around its middle.

"I know it's nothing you haven't seen before," Fifi said. "I would have gotten you a new car if I could have."

"You're giving me your car!"

He stroked the cherry red, the vanilla white, the silver chrome. It was like a sundae, like a valentine, like a little train, a magic carpet.

"Well, if you want it. Now that you can drive I thought it would be a good present. It's very safe. They made those things sturdy back then. And I'm getting a little too old to drive."

"I'll be your chauffeur. I love it, Grandma," Dirk said.

Then he noticed something different about the car. Mounted on the front was a golden thing.

"What's that?"

"It's a family heirloom. A lamp. It comes off the car, but for now I thought it looked splendid as a hood ornament."

"What's it for?"

"When you are ready you can tell your story into it," Fifi said. "You can talk about Pup—whatever you want to say. Secrets. Things you can't tell anyone."

"I don't have anything to say."

"Someday you may. Someday it might help."

Dirk looked at the golden thing. He was afraid of it. He wanted Fifi to take it back. But what could he do? Anyway, he had the car and that's what mattered. With the car he didn't need Pup; he didn't need anybody. He could drive through the canyons with the top down, race along Mulholland's precarious curves, looking at the city glistering below. He could feel the breeze kissing his naked temples, more tender than any lover. Go to punk gigs by himself. Slam in the pit with the boys until the pain sweated out of him, let the pain-sweat dry up and evaporate in the night air as he drove and drove.

But Dirk didn't go out that night. Instead he lay alone in the darkness. His hands kept wandering over his body wanting to touch himself the way someone would rub a magic lamp in a fairy tale to make a genie appear. But Dirk pulled his hands away. He wanted to cut them off. He wanted to turn off his mind. He tried to think about Nancy Nance but all he could see was Pup Lambert.

Dirk remembered what Fifi had said to him. How could he tell his story, he wondered? He had no story. And if he did no one would want to hear it. He would be laughed at, maybe attacked. So it was better to have no story at all. It was better to be dead inside.

He looked up at the billboard models looming above like hard angels in denim as he drove down the Sunset Strip one night. I would rather have no story at all, Dirk decided. I want to be blank like a model on a billboard. I want to be untouchable and beautiful and completely dead inside. But he thought of the stuffed dog he and Pup had seen on the Venice boardwalk, so long ago it seemed now—a rigor mortis display. Without a story of love would he become only that?

Dirk was going to see X at the Whiskey A-Go-Go. He had a fake ID he had made himself using his new driver's license. He had a black leather motorcycle jacket covered with zippers that he had found at a musty dusty cobwebs-and-lace thrift store for only ten dollars. He had his warrior

Mohawk. Kaboodle was sitting next to him on the front seat with gel in his shock of hair and his big paw resting on Dirk's leg.

The dark club was full of pierced, painted boys with shaved heads. They were slamming in the pit in front of the stage, throwing their bodies against each other in a wild-thing rumpus. Dirk felt that he fit in here much better than at school. Exene wove around with her two-tone hair hanging over her eyes and her arms and legs sticking out of her little black dress like the limbs of a doll that had been thrown around too much. John Doe's face looked even whiter against his black hair as he twisted it into expressions of torture and ecstasy, baring his teeth or pouting like James Dean. Billy Zoom's platinum ice devil smile never left his lips as he played his guitar at crotch level. The music made Dirk think of black roses on fire. He wanted to leap onstage and dive into the crowd the way some of the boys were doing. He wanted to play music that would make the boys in the pit sweat like that. Maybe that was how those boys cried, Dirk thought. Maybe he would start a band called the Tear Jerks. For a moment he remembered sitting in his room with Pup, Pup holding the guitar, but he let the drums beat the thought away. His own band. Dirk and the Tear Jerks. Tear Jerk Dirk.

His throat and heart felt tight, constricted with dryness, so he bought a beer and gulped it down. Then he went and stood at the edge of the slammers. Some boys behind him were moving up and down in place, jostling him forward. Finally he flung himself into the writhing body mass. It was like surfing in a way, fighting to stay up above seething waters that wanted to consume you, part of you wanting to be consumed, to vanish into radiance.

"The world's a mess it's in my kiss," X sang.

Dirk felt the bitterness and anguish making his lips tingle. He raged arms and legs akimbo into the fury. He was carried forward by the whirlpools of the crowd to the stage. On the stage. Blinded sweat tears lights. Howling. Panic. Pandemonium. Pan, hooved horned god. Flinging himself off into space. Waiting for the fall, the hard smack, unconsciousness.

No. Buoyed up. Thrilling sweat-slick biceps. Cradled for a moment. Father. Father. Objects in flight around the room. Fragments of poetry. Lost eyes far away. Eyes like boats drifting farther and farther away.

He was back on his feet again. The crowd had caught him. He had felt their respect and admiration. He wiped off sweat with the back of his hand and went to get another beer. As he walked through the crowd he felt some bodies move back to give him room, witness his strength, others brush against him to feel it. The lights caught zipper metal and raven hair. Sweat on tan skin like beer drops brown glass glisten.

After the show Dirk gave Kaboodle some water and

walked him until he peed. A boy and girl with matching burgundy hair that stood straight up on their heads like flames smiled at them.

"Mohawk dog," the boy said. "You're twins." Dirk and Kaboodle smiled back.

They got in the car and drove by Oki Dogs on Santa Monica Boulevard. Punks, kids with long greasy hair and junky-bulky veins in shriveled arms, tall men with big cars and sharp teeth, sat on the scarred benches under fluorescent lights that buzzed like flies or fat cooking. Dirk stopped the Pontiac and got out. The man at the counter shouted at him, "Okay okay," so he just said, "Oki Dog and a Coke." The Oki Dog was a giant hot dog smothered with cheese and beans and pastrami slices and wrapped in a tortilla. Dirk ate a few bites. It tasted salty greasy rich dark danger like the night. He was so hungry.

Then he saw a shrink-wrap swastika earring. It was dangling from the ear of a girl with spikey hair. The girl was drinking a Coke and giggling with her friends. She could have been Tracey or Nancy with a punk haircut.

"Do you know what that earring means?" Dirk said. He had never spoken out like this but suddenly his nerves felt huge, fluorescent, explosive. Maybe from the music still in his head. Maybe from the symbol.

The girl giggled. "It's a punk thing."

"Do you know who Hitler was?" Dirk asked.

"Yeah sure."

"Really? You know about the concentration camps?"

"Kind of. I guess. Why?"

"Hitler massacred innocent people. I'm sure you heard about it sometime. That was his symbol. The swastika."

"I got it at Poseur. It's cool."

"It is so uncool. You can't even believe how uncool it is," Dirk said.

The girl lowered her eyes. She looked to her friends and back to Dirk.

Dirk left Oki Dogs and got in his car. Kaboodle kissed his face and Dirk gave him the rest of the Oki Dog. As they drove away Dirk saw the girl pull the earring out of her ear and look at it.

So maybe it wasn't what he thought, this scene. But it was a wild enough animal safari that his own beastliness might go unnoticed.

He drove over the city's shoulders tattooed with wandering, hungry children and used car lots, drove past hanging traffic light earrings into beery breath mist, up and up above the city, trying to shed it like a skin. On the city's shaved head was the crown of the Griffith Observatory. The viewing balcony was closed, but the star Dirk had come to see was the bronze bust of James Dean on its pedestal. He gazed into its light and would have exchanged his soul for that boy's if he could.

Because he couldn't give his soul to James Dean, Dirk kept going out. Just keep going out, he told himself.

The Vex was a club in an old ballroom. Dirk drove into the parking lot under a freeway, concrete shaking like an earthquake. Inside there was a long curved bar and columns and balconies and chandeliers but everything looked ready to crumble from age and the freeway vibrations. Dirk watched a boy and girl slamming. The boy threw the girl down on the ground. She was wearing a lot of metal that shocked against the wood of the floor. He started hitting her in the face. Finally some guys broke it up but to Dirk it seemed like it went on forever. There was blood the color of her lipstick on the girl's face.

Dirk felt the piece of pizza he had eaten for dinner hot in his throat and ran into the bathroom. When he looked up under the greenish-white chill of the lights, his head felt as if he had slammed it against porcelain.

After that, Dirk drove along Sunset to the Carney's hot dog train.

"Do you have a dollar?" The boy sitting in front of Carney's looked like Sid Vicious. "I'm Sinbad," he said.

He was really skinny so Dirk motioned for him to follow him in. But when they were sitting on the bench outside, Sinbad said he didn't want the hot dog Dirk had bought.

"I'm a vampire," he said.

"A what?"

"A vampire."

He bared his teeth. He had fangs.

"They're bonded on," he said. "They really work. Want to see?"

"No," Dirk said.

"Don't you want to exchange blood with me?" He leaned closer on the bench.

"Get away from me," said Dirk.

"You don't know what might happen," said Sinbad.

Two boys walked by, leaning against each other, sharing a frozen yogurt.

"If you ask me all those fags are going to die out," said Sinbad.

As he got in his car, wishing he had brought Kaboodle for a kiss and a wink, Dirk thought of Sinbad's eyes. They were familiar. Where had he seen them? Then Dirk knew he had seen those eyes in the mirror when he scrutinized his face for blemishes and imperfections, when he imagined that no one would ever love him.

Fifi was volunteering at a local hospital the next night. Dirk was home listening to his Adolescents album.

"I hate them all—creatures."

The angry voice made Fifi's collection of plaster Jesus statues shake as if there were an earthquake, or as if they were about to start slamming, Dirk thought. He imagined a pit full of slamming plaster Jesuses. He didn't like the thought.

Suddenly Fifi's music box with the ballerina on top began to play, the ballerina going around and around on one toe. The china cabinet doors flew open and Fifi's coaster collection spun out like tiny Frisbees. Dirk covered his head to protect himself. The clown paintings on the walls swung back and forth, and Dirk thought he heard them laughing evil clown laughter. Dirk had never liked the clowns. He turned away from their leering mouths and saw the plaster Jesus statues slamming. Dirk stared into the eyes of one of them. The eyes were glowing. The statue fell from the shelf and its head broke off but the eyes kept sizzling like fried eggs. Finally the Adolescents' song was over and the house was quiet. Dirk heard an owl hooting in a branch outside the window and some cats screaming. He could have screamed like that. He plucked his wet T-shirt away from his sweating body and collapsed on the bed.

Fear, the band, was playing out in the valley. Dirk armed himself in chains and the leather motorcycle jacket. He rode the 101. The freeway made him think of loss instead of hope, stretching out under a hovering orangish buzz of night air, not seeming to lead anywhere. At night the valley felt deserted. Dirk drove down barren streets under tall streetlamps. The little houses looked blank, as if they wanted to deny that anything unpleasant happened in or around them, but the way they were nestling under the crackling telephone wires, Dirk knew they were afraid.

Dirk got to the place where Fear was. Punks were hanging out in the parking lot drinking beers, smoking, grimacing—everything out of the sides of their mouths. White-bleached hair bright under the blue lights, black-dyed hair stiff with hair spray, ears and noses pierced with metal, backs covered with leather. Some boys were giving each other tattoos with ink and needles. One boy was burning his arm with a cigarette butt while a girl shrieked at him. Dirk couldn't tell if she was laughing or crying.

He went inside. The lead singer's square white head and hate-filled mouth seemed blown up, larger than life. As the music speeded, Dirk climbed out of the pit, up onstage and flung himself into the slamming mash of bodies. As he fell into the sweating arms he felt desire inside and around him but it was a brutal thing, feverish and dangerous. He looked into the eyes of one boy and saw that the desire was mixed with a hate so deep it had the same shape as the swastika tattoo on the side of the boy's vein-corded neck. Dirk knew there was nothing he could say to the boy that would change what he thought about the thing inked so deep into his flesh, inked so deep into him. It wasn't like shrink wrap. But he said it anyway.

"Fuck fascist skinhead shit."

Swastika and two other boys with the same tattoo followed Dirk outside when the show was over.

"Where you going, faggot?" the first boy said.

Dirk felt they had looked inside of him to his most terrible secret and it shocked him so much that he lost all the quiet strength he had been trying to build for as long as he could remember.

"Fuck you," he whispered.

The skinheads were on him all at once. Dirk saw their eyes glittering like mica chips with the reflection of his own self-loathing. He wondered if he deserved this because he wanted to touch and kiss a boy. The sound of everything was so loud and he kept seeing the skinhead skulls with the stubble, the bunches of flesh at the back of the neck like a bulldog's. His own head felt like a shell. A thin one you could crush on the beach. He had never realized how delicate his head was. This pain was hardly different from what he had always felt inside—torn, jarred, pummeled. In a way it was a relief—a confirmation of that other pain. But he wanted to escape it all finally.

He wanted to die.

When the blood had stopped pouring enough for him to see, Dirk drove home. He never knew, later, how he made it. He had to stop every so often to lean his head against the wheel. Blood was all over the car upholstery.

Once when he looked up from the steering wheel he saw a house crossing the road. It was a cheerful-looking yellow house moving on wheels through the valley night. Dirk thought at first he must be hallucinating. Then he thought, my father. He didn't know why but that was what he thought. He leaned his head back down and when he looked up the house was gone.

When he got home finally he managed somehow to get the lamp Fifi had given him off the front of the car and carry it inside. He staggered to the bathroom and washed the gashes on his face while Kaboodle whimpered at his feet and gently pawed his leg. His reflection pitched and blurred in the mirror. Blood was caking now, turning darker and thicker.

Dirk steadied himself by leaning against the wall until he got to his bed. He fell down there and closed his eyes.

Dirk dreamed of the train. It was moving through the hills, through the forests like a thought through his mind, like blood through a vein in him. There were the fathers taking their showers. They were naked and close together under the water. But something was different. Thin fathers. Emaciated bodies. Shaved scalps. Something was happening. What was happening? Not water. Gas. Coming through the pipes. Gas to make their lungs explode. Dying fathers as the train kept going kept going kept going. To hell.

Part II

Gazelle's Story

it was lying over Dirk's heart staring at him, her usually aloe-vera-green eyes now black with pupil. Even Kit could not take away the pain flashing and shrieking through Dirk's body like an ambulance. His blood shivered.

Help me; tell me a story, Dirk thought, knowing that somewhere in the room the lamp was waiting. Tell me a story that will make me want to live, because right now I don't want to live. Help me.

He shut his eyes.

The wind was tapping the peach tree's long thin leaf fingers against the window. The moon cast shadows of the branches across the floor. Dirk sat up in bed and Kit jumped off of him, yowling. It felt as if Dirk's heart leaped out of his body with her. In the corner of the room beside the golden lamp the figure of a woman was seated on a chair. She was wearing a long dress of creamy satin covered with satin roses and beads that shone like crystals under rushing water, raindrops in the moonlight. There was a veil over her face but Dirk could see her pallor, the sadness in her eyes. Eyes like his own. He clutched his wild-duck-printed flannel pajama shirt closer around his chest impulsively but he was no longer cold. And the pain was far away now—a fading red light, a retreating siren.

Am I alive? Dirk wondered.

He wished that the woman would go away. But she looked so sad; she looked as though she needed to talk to him.

"Who are you?" Dirk said softly into the darkness.

"My name is Gazelle Sunday. You want me to go."

"No I don't."

Was she about to cry? Dirk didn't want her to. He tried to think of something.

"Do you have a story?" Dirk asked.

"A story?"

"Yeah. I don't have one."

"I can't remember," she said.

"I bet you can. I bet you are full of stories. I can see in your eyes."

"No, no, not really."

"Try to think." He really wanted her to tell him something now. "Maybe something about that dress. Where did you get that dress?"

The woman reached her almost-transparent hand out to him.

"Please," he said.

"If you will dance with me."

"Okay," said Dirk, and then wondered if that was such a good idea. She looked like death. He wondered if she would dance away with him. Dance him to his grave. Maybe that was the best thing. Maybe that was what he wanted. Or it had happened already. And besides he had promised, and she, this white ghost lady, had begun to tell.

"I never knew my mother but I knew she had given me my name and I loved her for that. I imagined that my mother and father were from France, very young, very in love. In my mind they looked like children in the book of fairy tales—the only thing besides my name that my mother had left me. The book was big and full of intricate, jewel-colored pictures of castles with turrets, enchanted mossy forests, goblins, banshees, trolls, brownies, pixies, fairies with huge butterfly wings and djinns on magic carpets. I pretended that the two children in one story were my parents. I saw them walking into the woods, their faces as pale as the snow they trudged through, their eyes big, dark mirrors like the frozen lakes they had to cross, their mouths like petals ripped from the red roses that they waited for all winter but never saw again, dying in each other's arms when I was born. At least that is the story I told myself, walking in circles, twisting my hair around one finger, sucking my lower lip, holding the book open in my arms.

"I lived with my aunt in a dark and musty building. The kitchen smelled of boiled cabbage and potatoes; the claw-foot bathtub behind the screen in the kitchen corner smelled of mildew no matter how hard I scrubbed it clean. I was always leaning my head out the window to smell the bay, the baking bread, to hear the trolley car ringing its bell as it crested the steep hill. In the parlor was a dressmaker's mannequin. I was afraid that if I misbehaved the mannequin would attack me with the needles and scissors my aunt used to make dresses.

"My aunt was a cold woman with raw hands and a mouth that looked as if it was always full of pins. She hated me. I knew that the only reason she let me live with her at all was because I helped her sew. I became a better and better seamstress. I could do the most elaborate embroidery and beadwork with my tiny fingers. I could make roses out of silk; they looked so real you hallucinated their fragrance. Women came from all over the city for my dresses. My aunt never let me wear what I made. I had one black frock and a brown one for Sunday church—the only day she let me out of the house. I didn't mind the hard work, really, or the plain clothes or even the fact that I couldn't leave and had no friends. But I wanted to dance. I needed it. Dancing was the only thing I wanted. I would do it in secret. With a child's wisdom I knew never to let my aunt see. She thought it was a sin."

That's like me, Dirk thought. Like me loving boys, not wanting anyone to know.

"When she went out I pulled back the carpets. It was very strange. Whenever she went out some beautiful music would start to play in the apartment next door. I learned later that it was Chopin. It was like a magical being from my fairy book had entered my body when I heard the music. I felt the strong center of who I was pulsing with the sound of those fingers on the piano keys; it radiated out through my limbs until I became like a giant butterfly or a silk rose, a waterfall, fire. I never saw anyone come out of the next-door apartment but it didn't matter—the gift of their music made me feel I had finally found a friend. I danced wildly the story of my parents, of my birth, my life with my aunt. I saw worlds beyond the parlor as if I were soaring through the air on a magic carpet, cities twinkling like fairies or the crowns of giants, and forests green and singing with elves."

In just the way that Gazelle had seen those cities and forests, Dirk saw, there before him, a Victorian parlor and a slim girl dancing among coffinlike furniture draped in dark shawls. She had a child's body in old-fashioned white underwear but her eyes and mouth were a woman's. She was spinning as if she wanted to make herself dizzy, falling to the floor where she twisted and turned and tangled in her pale hair, each motion full of longing. Dirk heard, too, the faint strains of piano music ghosting the air.

"I danced till I was nauseous and sweating through my underthings," Gazelle went on. "I had to change before my aunt came home. I knew she was coming because the music always stopped in time for me to change and get back to work. But one day even when the music stopped I kept dancing. I couldn't stop. I heard the music inside of me still. So that when my aunt came into the room I didn't even look up. I was kneeling on the floor, running my hands all over my body. Then I opened my eyes and I realized there hadn't been music for quite a while. My aunt was looking at me with scissors in her eyes.

"She grabbed my arm and pulled me to my feet.

"'What were you doing?' she said as if she were snipping pieces out of the air.

"I told her I was dancing.

"'Do you know what happens to girls like you?' my aunt said.

"I saw the mannequin in the corner. The cloth I had covered it with had slipped off. I imagined that the mannequin had needles sticking out of her body and

54

was ready to shoot them across the room at me.

"'Girls who touch themselves grow up ugly,' my aunt said, like a curse. 'No one will ever marry you. No one will want you because you will be a little monster. You are the devil's bride. He plays music in your head.'

"And it was worse than being whipped. It was as if she had broken my legs with that. I never heard the music again. I never danced. I never told my story.

"When I bled for the first time a few months later my aunt saw the stains on my underthings and said, 'You see. You see what happens to girls who touch themselves. They bleed like little monsters. But they don't die. You will wish you died, I think, because you will always be alone.'"

"Oh my God," Dirk said. "How could she do that to you? She was sick."

Gazelle wrung her hands. She was trembling.

"Are you cold?" Dirk asked her. He took a blanket off the bed and held it out.

"Oh, no thank you. How kind you are. Kind, like him."

"Who?" Dirk asked.

Gazelle's eyes filled with tears. "He saved me, finally. I thought I was a monster. I huddled and hunched in my black dress. My fingers cramped like an old woman's. My face grew twisted with pain. There were always bruise-blue circles under my eyes from holding my tears back. Without my dancing I was like the mannequin in the corner, no arms or legs, swaddled and bound. I never left the apartment.

"But he came to me finally. It was my sixteenth birthday, and my aunt was out. It was a windy evening full of spirits. I almost thought I heard my piano player through the walls but it was only the wind. There was a knock on the door."

As she spoke, Dirk saw the parlor again, the image quivering as if behind smoke or water. The girl was older this time, and her body looked as if it had never danced and never would. Dirk gasped to see how different she was, almost as ravaged as the woman in white. He wished he could have waltzed with her out of that place.

She hobbled over to a door and opened it. There stood a small man with dark skin and blue eyes. His head was shaved so that his sharp cheekbones seemed to stick out even more.

"I shivered with awe when I saw him. I felt my whole life lived in that moment—blooming from a seed in my mother's belly, swimming like a tiny slippery fish, growing a birdlike skeleton, clawing forth—a baby lynx, dancing as a girl, becoming a woman with a child inside of me, lying in a satin-lined coffin beneath the earth while a young woman danced the story of her life above me.

"'I need you to make a dress for my beloved,' said the man in a voice like a purr.

"'Come in,' I said.

"He sat on the brown sofa. I noticed a red jewel embedded in his nose. It caught the light like a tiny fire.

"'I want you to make me the most beautiful dress,' he went on. He reached into the sack he was carrying—he must have had a sack of some kind although I don't really remember it now. But how else could he have brought the fabric in? I remember the fabric. It was a bolt of thick cream Florentine satin. And he also gave me the most fragile lace—all chrysanthemums and peonies and lilies and baby's breath—and a golden box full of tiny crystal beads.

"He put all these things in front of me.

"'I'll need to see the woman in order to make it,' I said. I imagined a fairy woman with dark skin and pale eyes like his, jewels in her ears and nose and on her fingers, chunks of rubies, emeralds and sapphires like her eyes. I would have been afraid to touch a woman like that—to have her there at my fingertips, just on the other side of the satin, vulnerable to my pins and needles. But I wanted to see her, too.

"'I want the dress to be a surprise for her' was all he would say.

"'Do you have her dress size and measurements?' I

asked. I was very shy. I kept my head down the whole time I spoke to him. But I had to look up to see his answer because he was silent, just shaking his head and looking at me.

"'Well, how will I know what size to make it?'

"His eyes on me were like the softest touch, a touch I had not known since the last time I let my own hands caress my now monstrous, bleeding body, since the last time I danced. They were the color of blue ball-gown taffeta.

"'Looking at you . . . I think she is just your size,' he said.

"I blushed so much that I thought I was the color of the ruby in his nose. How could he know about my body beneath the black shawl I wore bundled around me? But I agreed to make the dress.

"Then he left. I almost danced again. I did dance in a way—my fingers danced over the satin. I sat at the black-and-gold sphinx sewing machine and made a ballet of a dress—the most beautiful dress. When I was finished he came back. My aunt was away. He asked me to put the dress on.

"I went into the back bedroom, so dim and draped in dark fabrics to keep out the light, and I put on the dress. The satin against my skin made me want to weep. The dress felt cool and warm, light and soft, supple and strong the way I imagined a lover would feel. I looked at myself in the stained mirror and hardly recognized the gleaming woman, skin as pure and pale as the satin, eyes lit with the candleshine of the dress, lips moist with the pleasure of the dress, who stared back at me.

"I came out into the parlor and showed the stranger. He sat forward on the sofa and looked at me with a hypnotic blue gaze.

" 'Thank you,' he said. I started to leave the room to change but he called me back. He put a large stack of bills on the table and rose to leave.

" 'Wait,' I said. 'Don't you want it? Isn't it right?'

" 'It is perfect.'

My eyes were full of questions.

" 'The dress is for you, Gazelle. And there is something else I want to give you.' "

Dirk watched Gazelle take the golden lamp to her breast as if it were a nursing child. "I asked him what it was," she said.

"What did he say?" Dirk whispered.

"That it was the place to keep my secrets, the story of my love. But I told him I have no story."

Like me and Fifi, Dirk thought.

"He said, 'Yes you do. We all do. Someday you will know it.' He started to leave then, and I brushed my fingers against his shoulder. His eyes looked into mine—big pale sky crystals full of sorrow and wisdom. Lakes full of first stars that I wanted to leap into, wishing.

"'Please,' I said.

"He took my hands in his. His hands weren't much bigger than mine but they were powerful and hot, the color of the cocoa velvet I used to sew winter hats. He put his lips to mine. I felt the room fill up with satiny light and a sweet powdery fragrance.

"'You must not be afraid' were the last words he said to me.

"The next month I didn't bleed. At first I thought that my aunt's curse was over—I wasn't a monster anymore, I had been good. But when my belly got bigger and bigger I thought that her curse had become even more powerful.

"'Oh, I knew you were evil,' she said. 'It must be the devil's child. Who else could have touched you? Who else would have touched you?'

"I thought about the stranger. Could he have been the devil? If he was the devil I would have gone with him anyway. I wished he would come back."

"How could she say those things to you?" Dirk asked. "What happened? Did you have your baby?"

"Yes. She told me we would put it up for adoption when it was born. And she locked me in my room so the women who came over for fittings wouldn't see me. She only opened the door to give me food and the material to sew. I wanted to die. I might have killed myself with the sewing shears except for three things—the baby inside of me, the magical dress hidden in mothballs and tissue in my closet and the words I heard purring through my head. 'You must not be afraid.'

"Then just before my baby was born my aunt fell ill. She let me out of my room, and I sat at her bedside pressing damp lavender-soaked rags to her forehead and feeding her soft food."

"You should have strangled her," Dirk said. "Sorry. But I think she deserved it."

"She was a damaged woman. I would have been too if the stranger hadn't come. Someone had seen her touch herself, maybe even seen her dance, and told her those horrible lies."

Dirk said, "You're kinder than I am," and she answered, "No, not really. I was just trying to protect my baby, you know. I remembered all the fairy tales about the evil witch cursing the child. She'd almost destroyed me, and I wasn't going to let her hurt the baby."

"Did she?"

"No. She died rather peacefully with my hands on her temples. Poor thing, I think I might have been the first one to touch her all those years."

"Then what happened?"

"I gave birth to the most beautiful little girl! The most perfect little girl. She had tiny naturally turned-out feet and fluttering pink hands like wings and she danced everywhere. From the moment she came out of me she was dancing."

Dirk saw the phantom parlor again, although this time the walls were freshly painted white; the floral friezes along the ceiling were pale pink and blue. Lace curtains like bridal veils hung at the open windows. He thought he heard the piano music again.

"I painted the inside of the house and kept the windows open all day," Gazelle said. "I sewed large floral tapestry cloth pillows, pink, blue and gold, and stuffed them with dried lavender and rose petals. I re-covered the brown sofa in jade-green velvet. I made a chiffon canopy over the bed and lit long tapers so that through the draperies the house looked full of stars. I built fires in the fireplace that my aunt never used, and the house smelled of cedar smoke. I read poetry aloud—Shelley and Keats. 'The silver lamp—the ravishment—the wonder. The darkness—loneliness—the fearful thunder,' only it was a golden lamp and there was no more darkness.

"My daughter, who loved to draw, made a picture of a lovely face and put it on the mannequin under a big hat covered with birds' nests full of pale blue eggs.

"'Now you won't be afraid of her anymore,' she said, child-wise.

"No longer prisoners, we went out into the city that had been forbidden to me for so long. We walked up and

62

down the hills until our legs ached, then rode the trolley car to feel rushes of salty, misty air. We had picnics and fed the swans on the lake under the flowering terra-cotta arches, drank tea and ate pastries in rooms with cupids and rosebuds painted on the walls, strolled through the park, green-dazzled, fragrance-drunk, gasped at treasures gleaming gold in the half-lit glass cases of the museum. Then we'd return with spices, fruits and vegetables from Chinatown, seafood and baguettes from the wharf.

"The piano music began again—coming through the walls every evening—and I watched my child dance. It was almost as if I were dancing myself. She danced among the spools of thread, the ribbons and laces, the silk flowers.

"After a while I took her for ballet lessons from Madame Joy. I brought her to the studio four times a week. She was the littlest in class but the very best; everyone thought so. I made her a garland of silk blossoms and some tiny pink net wings. She always played sprites or pixies in the dance recitals. I sat and watched her with such pride.

"Sometimes, though, she wouldn't stick to the chore-ography. She couldn't help it, she'd just start doing her own dances. Madame Joy hated that.

"'What are you doing, idiot-child!' she screamed.

"She took her cane and hooked it around my baby's

waist; she hit it against her backside. I was mortified when I found bruises on her.

"'I don't want you going back there,' I said. 'You can dance at home.'

"But I knew she missed performing. I sat and watched her for hours, shining a light on her, but it wasn't the same.

"One day when we were walking down the street she started to jump up and down, tugging my fingers and pointing. Two little boys in spangled blue costumes were taking turns balancing on each other's shoulders in front of a crowd. She let go of my hand and before I could stop her she had jumped into the act, climbing up the tree of the boys to pose on top like a Christmas angel. They made her spin like a music box ballerina. The crowd cheered. I was so proud. After that Fifi joined the act."

"Fifi!" Dirk said.

"Yes. Your grandmother."

"I didn't know all this about her childhood," Dirk said. "Or about you." He was embarrassed that he hadn't even heard Gazelle's name before.

"That's because you never asked."

Dirk knew that was true. He had just assumed that Fifi was always a spun-sugar-haired grandmother living in the cottage, alone.

"And she never asked about my life," Gazelle said.

"And I never asked about my aunt's. That's the way children are sometimes. Until its too late. If I had asked my aunt about herself it might have helped her. It's important to tell your story. It's important to listen."

"Tell me more," Dirk said.

"The years went by. Fifi danced with Martin and Merlin, first on the street and then in cafés. Everyone thought that either Martin or Merlin was her beau so Fifi never had any gentleman callers. Sometimes I would find her crying into the tulle and silk of her dancing costume.

"'What's wrong?' I would ask her. 'Your dress will be so heavy with tears the boys won't be able to lift you.'

"No man will like me,' she said. 'I'm such a cricket, an insect.'

"'Don't say those things,' I scolded. I was afraid that somehow I had passed on to her the self-hatred my aunt had given me, although I was always telling her what a great beauty she was and that her size only added to it. Still, she did her stretches diligently, hoping they would make her taller. She wore the highest heels she could find, although I warned her about her feet, and did exercises to increase her bustline.

"I told her that I thought people believed she was engaged to Martin or Merlin, that she might not encourage that so much, but she wouldn't hear of it. She always held their arms when they walked down the street and let them introduce her as their fiancée sometimes. It was her way of protecting them, you see. In those days their feelings for each other weren't something people talked about. Of course, it was quite obvious to me. When they performed they would hand her back and forth between them like a love letter."

"Like a love letter," Dirk said.

"Yes. They loved each other."

"I know," said Dirk. "What do you think about that?"

"Any love that is love is right," Gazelle said. "It's the same as me touching myself when I was a child. Do you understand?"

"Yes," Dirk said. "I understand." Something in his body opened like a love letter. He wondered if Fifi would understand about him. . . . Maybe she had all along.

Gazelle went on.

"Fifi always played along with being engaged to Martin or Merlin, depending on whose relatives were at the show. But it enforced the feeling that no man would love her the way she dreamed of being loved. She became more shy, staying home all day drawing and painting in the parlor. Sometimes we went to the countryside where she set up an easel and painted the fields full of cows, the wildflowers and redwoods. She loved color. She used to say how she would paint everything if she could, eat orange or green porridge, cover the ceiling with flowers, make her hair pink or purple."

"Fifi the original punk," Dirk said. "She just needed a man as wild as she was."

"Well, she found him. One night she was performing at a supper club. As she left the theater in her gold brocade coat, peach roses in her hair, she was stopped by a tall, dark, sad-eyed man. He tipped his hat to her and a hundred fireflies came swarming out, surrounding her and lighting her up as if she were still on stage."

"'How did you learn that?' she gasped.

"'I'm an entomologist,' he said. 'But magic like this only happens when you meet your true love. My name is Derwood McDonald.'"

"McDonald," Dirk said. "My grandfather. He was a bug guy?"

"That's right," said Gazelle. "I wouldn't call him a bug guy. He was a magician really."

"That's what the bug ambulances are about, I guess," Dirk said. "When Grandma Fifi finds an insect in the house she gets an old yogurt container or something and makes this siren noise. She puts the bug into it and takes it outside. She calls it a bug ambulance."

"That's my daughter," Gazelle said. "Anyway, just then her partners appeared and took her arms.

"Derwood McDonald introduced himself to them and

added, 'I was going to ask you to dinner, Fifi, but you look as if you already have plans.'

"She told him she didn't have plans, that she saw Martin and Merlin every day and every night.

"'It's true,' they agreed, nodding in unison. From all their performances they had become accustomed to moving as one.

"'Fifi might enjoy some new company.' They bowed and walked off, side by side.

"By the time Fifi and Derwood got to the restaurant there were so many ladybugs on Derwood's jacket collar that they looked like red polka dots.

"'You must have very good luck,' she said.

"'I am having it now,' he answered.

"They ate pasta and drank red wine. She told him about her dancing, how she loved to draw and had started to take art classes.

"'I won't always be able to do those adagio tricks,' she said. 'I'm trying to plan for my future.'

"He told her, 'You will probably dance when you are ninety years old. You remind me of the fairies I saw in the countryside when I was a boy. My father—he was a naturalist too—pointed them out to me as if they were just another form of insect so I never understood why people thought they were made up. They had wings like large honeysuckle blossoms and were finger-size, but otherwise you look just like one. After I grew up I thought I'd never see another fairy,' he said. 'Until I laid eyes on you. Are you a fairy, Fifi?'

"Fifi giggled. Derwood laughed too but his fairy-filled eyes remained sad.

"He walked her home. She came into the house flushed and happier than I had ever seen her. I thought of the night the stranger had come to my door.

" 'What is it, Fifi?' I asked.

"She knew even then that she loved him, that she wanted to marry him.

"On Sundays Derwood took Fifi to the countryside. They caught butterflies in a net, studied the beautiful paintings of their wings and set them free. When Derwood found dead butterflies he would take them home and make collages that he framed behind glass. He and Fifi looked for fairies too, but never found any.

" 'It doesn't matter," Derwood said as she came back with dirt on her hands and leaves in her hair from searching through grottos and barrows. 'You are my fairy.'

"In the evenings Derwood came calling with honey from his bees. It tasted like nothing less than nectar made for the love of a golden queen by a hundred droning drones. We slathered it on homemade bread, drizzled it over rice pudding, let big shining drops fall into our teacups and blended it into sauces for the salmon we ate on Fridays. I played the phonograph and Fifi danced. Sometimes Martin and Merlin came over too and they all performed for us. Derwood sat on the jade-green sofa among the rose- and lavender-stuffed pillows wringing his hands during the most precarious balances, clapping and stomping when a trick had been executed.

"But as much as Fifi loved Derwood I could tell something was wrong.

"Finally, after Fifi had known him for a few months and he still hadn't kissed her, she asked him what it was.

"'I have a heart condition,' he told her. 'The doctors tell me I only have a few more years to live.'

"Fifi wanted to run away from him.

"Derwood said, 'I will understand if you don't want to see me anymore.'

"Fifi broke into tears but her sobs sounded like the flicker of crickets. Hundreds of ladybugs flew and landed on her hat. Cocoons opened and butterflies were released in a storm. She held on to Derwood in the forest of wings, and a golden powder covered their faces. Fifi was afraid they would be suffocated, but the butterflies only seemed to be kissing their cheeks.

"'I want to be with you, Derwood McDonald,' Fifi said. 'No matter what.'

"A golden ring slid down out of the air and moved across the picnic cloth toward Fifi. She gasped when she saw the two tiny ring bearers.

"'These are my pet spiders, Charlotte and Webster,'

Derwood said. 'They want to know if you will marry me.'

"Not wanting to waste a moment, Fifi and Derwood were married the next day. Fifi wore the dress I had made for the stranger. Hundreds of pink doves flew alongside Derwood's car on the way home.

"Derwood and Fifi lived in a gingerbread house a few blocks away from me. It had two tall columns in front and cherubs bearing garlands over the windows. It was painted lavender but it was like a greenhouse full of flowering plants, butterflies, crickets, doves. Thin sheets of tin, pressed with the patterns of ribboned urns full of cascading leaves, covered the walls. Derwood studied his insects by the light of the Tiffany lamp. Fifi, who was still taking art classes, drew the insects Derwood loved, and made them dance—balletic butterflies, tangoing tarantulas, waltzing caterpillars and tap-dancing bees.

"Fifi and Derwood hated to be separated, even for moments. Wherever they went they held hands. At night Fifi danced for him, swirling around in her glittery dresses, bringing tears of joy to Derwood's eyes.

"'I knew you were a fairy,' he said.

"Fifi peeked at him from behind a lavender ostrich-feather fan.

"Then I can make all your dreams come true."

"He took her in his arms and kissed her as the pink doves watched from the rafters and ladybugs and spiders and butterflies sang silently along with the radio. Fifi knew, though, that she and Derwood had only one dream and that she could not make it come true. It would take a much more powerful fairy than Fifi to cure what was wrong with Derwood's heart.

"At night she put her head on his lean chest and heard it ticking like an explosive. Fifi did make many of her dear Derwood's dreams come true before he died.

"'You make my dreams come true every night,' he whispered into her wispy hair as they fell asleep, fearless from the wine of love.

"And one night, Fifi knew that she was pregnant.

"'I'm pregnant,' she almost shouted.

"'You mean just this second?'

"'Yes.'

"'How do you know?'

"'I know. I'm a dancer. I've always known things about my body.'

"Derwood put his hand on her flat stomach. Her narrow waist and hips didn't look big enough to hold a baby. Fifi listened for Derwood's tears in the darkness. Instead she heard the soft, damp crackle of his smile.

"So she had made another of his dreams come true. His son, Dirby McDonald, your father.

"Dirby was born a very serious little boy. His father was afraid to get too close to him because he knew their time together would be so short. Fifi was so busy worrying about Derwood that she didn't give the child the attention he needed. I tried to care for him but he was always far away in his own world. He was a mystery to me.

"Finally one day, while Fifi and Derwood were out on one of their excursions to the countryside, Derwood sat down by the bank of a shallow, shimmering creek. A giant white butterfly flew past, and Fifi ran after it. She wanted to show it to Derwood. Maybe, she thought, the butterfly is really the fairy we have been looking for. But she couldn't catch it. When she got back to the creek Derwood was lying on his back. His face was covered with butterflies. They seemed to be trying to get inside of him or maybe they were coming out of him. But Derwood did not struggle. By the time Fifi had run to his side the butterflies were scattered and Derwood was dead. Fifi drove Derwood's car back to the house and collapsed on the front step before I had time to open the door with Dirby in my arms. There was Fifi lying in a heap. For a moment I didn't recognize her. Her hair was completely white. Dirby didn't cry. He just stared like an old man who has seen many deaths, his face tight and drawn. I put his white-haired mother to bed. She wouldn't eat for days. She seemed to be shrinking.

"'I never really believed he would die. I don't want to live without him,' she said.

"'You have to live, for Dirby and me,' I said, holding up her son for her to see. Oh, your father looked like you, young Dirk. He looked like his own father too.

"It made Fifi weep to see Derwood's eyes in that young face but she reached out for him, and when she did the doves in the rafters sang again, and the peonies in the arboretum unfolded layers and layers like Renaissance ruffs.

"'You see,' I said, 'you must hold on.'

"Her art school teacher sent her work to an animation department in Hollywood. They wanted to hire her.

"'I don't want to leave you, Mama,' she said. 'I stayed alive so I could be with you and Dirby.'

"I told her she had to go. 'There are groves of orange trees—you can pick your breakfast every morning—fountains in the hillsides, starlets in silk stockings driving colorful jalopies with leopards in the passenger seats, sunshine all the time. The sun will be good for Dirby. He's as pale as his old grandmother.'

"'You should come with us,' Fifi said, but I couldn't. I was afraid to travel and besides, what if my stranger returned and I was gone?

"So they prepared to leave, Fifi and Dirby with Martin and Merlin in a big old automobile with the glitter-and-paint dance backdrops of swans and heavens and circuses and fairylands fastened to the top.

"I gave Fifi the stranger's lamp as a good-bye gift. I

still didn't believe I had a story to tell. A self-imposed shroud of silence had covered me long before the real shroud of death made it impossible for me to speak. But my daughter would have a story, I thought; Fifi would fill the lamp.

"She didn't want to take it from me but I made her promise. Just before she was to leave, the story that I still did not believe was mine came to an end.

"And now it's time for you to dance with me," Gazelle said softly.

Dirk stood up slowly, aware of how light he felt, and held out his arms. She was like Fifi's feather boa—not only that weightless but she brushed his skin with ticklish flicks of softness. She smelled like his grandma too—cookies baking, roses, almonds. Gently, gently Dirk and his Great-Grandmother Gazelle danced around the room while the peach tree tapped at the window and the moon made a shadow forest on the floor. Dirk saw the story of her life repeated now with the sway of the white dress, the pleatings and swishings of satin.

"Thank you, Dirk," Gazelle said, when the dance was over. "Bless you. You listened. You listened."

Death came for me, Dirk thought. She was fading away as she had come and he thought he would dissolve with her, molecules shifting without substance into veil of spirit.

Be-Bop Bo-Peep

nd that was when the guitar in the corner began to play by itself.

Dirk opened his eyes. The guitar seemed to be floating on its side, strings trembling with music. Strands of smoke were flying out of the golden lamp and whirling around the guitar.

"Daddy," Dirk said out loud, remembering something he had lost a long time ago.

And Dirk's daddy Dirby McDonald's face appeared out of the smoke just above the guitar, as handsome as James Dean, not much older than Dirk, eyes soft with love like a lullaby behind his black-framed glasses. Lullaby eyes.

"Dirk," his father said, "hang on now."

Dirk nodded. He could taste blood in his mouth like he'd been sucking on a dirty metal harmonica.

"You came back," Dirk said.

"You want a story. A wake-up story. A come-back story."

"Yes. Please," Dirk said. "Please tell me who you are. I've always wanted to know. I feel like I don't exist. I feel like I'm spinning through space losing atoms, becoming invisible, disintegrating. I . . . ."

"Shhh, now," Dirk's father said. His voice was gentle. It was like his guitar. Like his eyes. Dirk thought, His eyes are guitars.

"What do you want to know?"

"What you felt. Who you were. Why you died."

"I always felt lonely," Dirby said. "It was just who I was born to be. I felt more like a part of nature than like a boy. Do you know what I mean?"

Dirk wasn't sure.

"I'd look at the stars in the sky or at trees and I'd want to be that. I worried Fifi. She was always trying to get me to be normal—play with the other kids, laugh more. She took me to her bungalow on the studio lot and showed me how she made the limbs of creatures move by drawing them again and again on clear sheets with light shining through. One of her projects was a story about herself and my father. The fireflies had devilish grins, the ladybugs had long eyelashes, the honeybees sang like Cab Calloway and the spiders danced like Fred and Ginger. She tried to get me to laugh, but I just asked questions about how butterflies hatched from cocoons and how spiders made their webs. I wanted to walk in the hills at night and get as close to the moon and stars as I could. I wanted to lie in the dark grasses of the canyon and listen to the wind play them like the strings of a guitar. I wrote poetry from the time I could write. That was the only way I could begin to express who I was but the poems didn't make sense to my teachers. They didn't rhyme. They were about the wind sounds, the planets' motion, never about who I was or how I felt. I didn't think I felt anything. I was this mind more than a body or a heart. My mind photographing the stars, hearing the wind. My forehead was lined before I was sixteen and I was always thin no matter how much Fifi tried to feed me."

Dirk looked at his father's body in the black turtleneck and jeans. Dirby's frame was just like Dirk's with the broad shoulders, narrow hips and long legs, but Dirk weighed at least fifteen pounds more and was lean himself.

"When my father died and I saw my mother's hair turn suddenly white I decided I was going to be like the clouds passing over the moon or the waves sliding up and back or the birds putting sounds together. That was the only way I could go on, accepting the way life was, being in the world.

"Then one night when I was sixteen I hitchhiked down into Topanga Canyon. I loved it there—the wild of it so near the sea, the thickness of trees and the smell of salt water all sharp and clean. I had to get away from the sugar smell in Fifi's kitchen and the roses; as much as I loved her I felt like I couldn't breathe—like it wasn't my world in any way.

"I walked inside this canyon bar and for the first time in my life I felt at home with walls around me. There was a cat onstage playing saxophone and chicks in black stockings sitting around watching him. There was beer and smoke—not just cigarettes, the kind of smoke that helps ease you into trees and wind. I knew I'd be coming back here.

"I came back all the time—every chance I could get away. All I needed was my thumb and my poetry journal. I also got a black turtleneck from my father's closet and a black beret from a thrift store so I'd look like the other cats hanging there in the mystic smoke and swinging sax night.

"One night a skinny old guy wearing shades asked me what I was writing in that journal all the time and I told him poetry.

"'You're a baby. What do you know about poetry?' he said, all languid-like.

"'I know enough,' I said.

"'Yeah. I bet you know some nursery rhymes. Little Bo-Peep come blow your horn the cat's in the meadow the chick's in the corn. That's poetry, right?'

"I tried to walk away from him but he called after me, 'That's poetry, right, Bo-Peep?'"

"After that everyone called me Bo-Peep. Until the night I got up on that stage, sat down on a stool in the moon of light and read what I'd been writing all those nights.

"Everyone got still, especially that old man. They leaned in close to dig the words. But it was more than words. Something was happening. There was this bottle of red wine and four glasses on the table next to me and they started dancing, I mean really dancing, doing some kind of tango-fandango number. Then the shades on the face of the old man jumped right off and started floating in the air, moving just out of his reach when he grabbed for them. I saw his eyes with the pinpoint pupils and red whites and knew why he wore those shades but there was nothing I could do about what was going on. I just kept reading. They were all digging it more and more, even the old guy. More stuff kept going on. My beret flew off my head and went slinging across the room onto the head of this beautiful chick. She had short hair like a boy's, almond-shaped eyes and breasts that were the shape of one of those stiff padded bras but I could tell, even from the stage, that she wasn't wearing one. She was wearing a black dress and black fishnet stockings on the longest legs I'd ever seen. She laughed and put her hands to her head where my beret had landed. Her girl friend handed her a joint but it didn't stay between her long fingers. It flew right out of those fingers and across the room, landing in my hand. I swear this is all true, buddy. Not that it sounds like the truth but it was."

Dirk was less stunned by the thought of his father's words making wineglasses dance than by what he saw hovering behind Dirby. When he saw her he remembered the way her long eyelashes had felt, ticklish as butterflies against his skin, he remembered the smoke of her voice and the patchouli smell in her hair, her long glamorous legs in black stockings. She was more beautiful than any girl in a magazine, she the boyish goddess. She was Edie Sedgwick and Twiggy and Bowie and like his father she was James Dean too. Just Silver. Mother. While Dirby kept talking she did a slow rhythmic dance, hands over her head, torso moving with sinuous snakey charm.

"Mom," Dirk said.

"After, I stopped reading my poetry, things settled down," Dirby went on. "I mean no more dancing wineglasses or flying joints, but everyone went wild.

"The old guy came up onstage—he had his shades again—and said, 'This, my friends, is Be-Bop Bo-Peep, beat guru.'

"I wanted to get out of there fast but the beautiful chick reached for my arm when I passed her table and put the beret back on my head. She smelled like incense and patchouli and orange blossoms. The light caught the big silver hoops she wore in her ears.

"'I dug that, Be-Bop,' she said.

"I just nodded the way I'd seen the hipsters do when someone dug them.

"'My name is Just Silver,' she said. 'Just Silver with a capital J capital S. The Just is because I renounced my father's name.'

"'Are you a model?' I asked.

"She was. An actress too. She had done little theater and had a tiny part in a Fellini film once.

"'You are very, very beautiful,' I told her. I knew I sounded more like Bo-Peep than Be-Bop talking like that but I felt she had dug right into my heart.

"She asked if I'd read *Siddhartha*. It was my favorite book. She told me I reminded her of him.

"'Come home with me,' she said.

"She drove me in her black convertible VW Bug to her apartment above the Sunset Strip. There was no furniture in the apartment—just rugs. Just Silver's family had traveled all over India and the Mideast purchasing rugs when she was a child. She lit some Nag Champra incense—flowers turned to powdery stick stems, turned to clouds of smoke petals—put on some Ravi Shankar and made her head move from side to side on her neck like an Indian goddess. Then she cooked vegetable curry

82

with rare saffron that was the color of poppy pollen.

"'Do you know what this is?' she asked, showing me a dancing metal goddess holding a severed head and wearing a necklace made of skulls.

"'I might think twice about getting into her car if I was hitching,' I said.

"'Would you really? I don't believe you.'

"'You're right. I'd get right in. She is beautiful.'

"'She's Kali, the blessing, dancing goddess. She's also death. In the East those things can go together.'

"I knew what she meant. She danced for me for a while and then we lay on her mattress and made love all night.

"After that I didn't feel any less lonely, only that Just Silver had joined me in the wild blue windscape of my loneliness.

"'I'm pregnant,' she said one night as I felt her draw me inside of her like a mouth on a pipe full of a burning dream-plant.

"'What? Just this second?'

"'Yes.'

"'How do you know?'

"'I am very in touch with my body.'

"'I can tell.'

"'What are we going to do?' She said we, knowing somehow that I wasn't going to leave even though I reminded her of Siddhartha.

"'I never had a dad,' I said.

"'I'm sorry. What happened?'

"'Well I had him for a while but he died when I was five. He knew he was going to die so even when he was alive he kind of ignored me.'

"Just Silver kissed the angles of my face. Her hair smelled like Nag Champra and marijuana. Her eyelashes were so long they looked like they hurt her. Her legs were as long as mine when we lay hip to hip and measured. Steep thighs.

"'So you don't want a baby,' Just Silver said. 'I mean, because of your dad.'

"'No. I want a baby because of my dad. I want a baby so I can be a dad for him.'

"'Or her,' Just Silver said.

"'I think we will have a boy.'

"'Why?'

"'I'm very in touch with our bodies.'

"'I can tell.'

"So we decided to have you, buddy. We almost named you Siddhartha but Fifi convinced us it was not going to be fun for a little boy to grow up with a name like Siddhartha, and Sid didn't have the right feeling. Fifi liked the name Dirk because of the sound of Derwood and Dirby and so we agreed, although your mother didn't see much difference between Dirk and Sid.

"Fifi loved your mom as if she were her very own

daughter. She was so happy to see me with a friend. I had really never had any friends. Now Just Silver and I went everywhere together. I would recite my poetry and she would do her interpretive dancing on the stage. The wineglasses danced with her. I had expected things to stop moving around when I fell in love but I was just as telekinetic as ever. Maybe more so. Instead of grounding me, my love sent me spinning even deeper into the center of loneliness that was the stars and the night and the wind. I didn't feel that my love was anything to do with the planet I had been born on. I wanted to fly away with Just Silver.

"Then you were born. You presented me with this problem. How was I supposed to keep living this abstract way, trying to be like music from a horn, like sweat, like the dark skin of night peeling back at dawn? Although I'd wanted a baby so I could love it the way my father hadn't been able to love me, when I saw you with your eyelashes and toes and everything, I realized what a big responsibility you really were. I had to care in a way I had never had to care before. I read you poetry and played my guitar. I made your toys fly around the room like planets in space. But I was drawn more and more to the waves and the wind. You made my heart hurt too much. It ached so much I thought it would stop pumping like my father's had.

"Your mother and I would leave you with your grandmother and go driving for hours. We liked to take Sunset all the way to the sea. We kissed in the furious Santa

Anas that felt like jewel dust whirling around us as the sun went down.

"The night we gave up on life, I can't say it was a conscious decision. But we didn't struggle against it either. That was the year Martin Luther King and Robert Kennedy were killed. In a way I think it was all too much for us—this world."

Dirk thought of his parents on the precipice, wanting to sink into the cavern of night and wild coyote hills, away from the hammering headlines and screaming TVs and the death of fathers.

"That's why I want you to be different, Dirk," said Dirby. "I want you to fight. I love you, buddy. I want you not to be afraid."

"But I'm gay," Dirk said. "Dad, I'm gay."

"I know you are, buddy," Dirby said. And his lullaby eyes sang with love. "Do you know about the Greek Gods, probably Walt Whitman—first beat father, Oscar Wilde, Ginsberg, even, maybe, your number one hero? You can't be afraid."

"Maybe it's too late," Dirk said. "Dad, am I alive now?"

"Yes. Still. Fight, Dirk."

"Mom?"

And then his mother, still dancing behind Dirby, all eyelashes and legs, spoke with that dream-plant smoke voice, "Tell us your story, Baby Be-Bop."

Genie

ne night when he was little Dirk McDonald woke to the sound of the telephone and his Grandma Fifi's voice," Dirk began.

"He had never heard a voice sound like that. Dirk looked up at the glow-in-the-dark stars Grandma Fifi had pasted on the ceiling for Dirk's father when he was a little boy. She had told Dirk they would keep nightmares away. But that night Dirk thought nothing would ever keep him safe from nightmares.

"Grandma Fifi ran into the bedroom and took Dirk in her arms. Her bones felt as light as the birdcage that hung in her kitchen. She wrapped him in a coat that smelled sour from mothballs and lilac-sweet from her perfume.

"Dirk sat huddled next to his grandmother in her red-and-white 1955 Pontiac convertible and felt as if the night was going to eat him alive; he wished it would. Fifi hadn't taken time to put the top back on. She ran through red lights. Dirk had never seen her do that before.

"When they got to the hospital a doctor met them in

the hallway and led them back into the waiting room. Fifi took Dirk on her lap. Dirk could never remember, later, if the doctor had ever said the words, but he knew then that his parents were gone. He pressed his face into the velvet collar of Fifi's coat and their tears mingled together until they were drenched with salt water.

"Dirk listened for his parents' voices in the wind sometimes. But soon he forgot what they had sounded like. All he could hear was his Grandma Fifi whistling with her canaries in the kitchen or calling to him to come out and play in the yard or asking the pastry dough what shape it intended on taking this afternoon or singing him lullabies."

Dirk went on to tell the story of life in Fifi's cottage, the fathers in the shower, the story of Pup Lambert and the magic lamp. He told the story of Gazelle and the stranger, Fifi and Derwood, Dirby and Just Silver. All his ancestors' stories were also his own.

Each of us has a family tree full of stories inside of us, Dirk thought. Each of us has a story blossoming out of us.

"Dad?" he asked the darkness. "Mom?" but Dirby and Just Silver were gone.

He picked up the golden lamp. It was heavy with stories of love. It was light with stories of love. It could sink to the bottom of the sea, touch the core of the earth with the weight of love. It could soar into the clouds like a creature with wings.

Just then he saw that the lamp had begun to smoke—

vapors writhing out from it like snakes. And Dirk saw emerging from that mist the face and then the whole body of a man. There was a piece of sapphire silk with golden elephants on it wrapped turban-style around his head. Dirk knew that beneath the turban, the man's scalp was shaved; he was the stranger who had come to Gazelle's door with the very lamp out of which he was now materializing.

"Come with me," the man said.

"Where?"

"You'll see."

The braid rug on the floor of Dirk's room began to quiver. Then the corners furled off the wooden floor and the rug lifted from the ground, bringing with it Dirk in his bed. Dirk closed his eyes the way you do on a roller coaster, wind and gravity forcing lids down, forcing him to grip the brass posts as the bed levitated. Eyes still closed but he knew he was outside now careening through star-flecked space on warm wind, part of him wanting to scream, wake from the dream, part of him letting this be, this journey to wherever, this journey on the voice of the man.

Beneath him the city the way it looked from inside the Japanese restaurant on the hill where waitresses in flowered silk kimonos brought starbursts and blossoms of sushi maki and champagne in silver ice buckets. A platter of gleaming wineglasses and luminous liqueurs, main courses served on polished plates, towering flaming desserts, candlelit birthday cakes. And on to the edges where it was darker and on to the sea that broke against the shore in seaweed black against iced jade pale. Dark waves becoming pale foam like the banks of wild dill and evening primrose growing along the highway. Ancient stone creatures emerging from the sea. Fields full of cattle. Some were there to die. He saw a bull mount a cow like a wave of life in the midst of static death. Fields full of farmworkers, sweat stories hidden behind the clustering clean sea green, sea purple of the grapes they picked. Redwood groves purple shadows light fallen like pollen through high leaves. Sea going so far it looks like sky. Just blues forever. Sky like a field of lupine and white wildflower fluffs. Sheer rivulets of water a skin of light over the sand. On and on. Where was he going?

In a field at the edge of the sea was a white house with crystals and lace in the window. Trumpet vines grew over the trellis and picket fence in front. A hammock in the garden. On the porch were surfboards, sandals, sleeping golden retrievers.

Duck Drake and his family lived in the house that smelled of beeswax and lavender and home-baked bread. Duck's mother Darlene had wide-apart green eyes, frothy yellow hair and petite tan legs. She liked to stand on the porch having long conversations with the mockingbird who lived in the garden. She was always asking Duck questions about what his favorite flower was and why and what was his favorite color and time of day and animal and what dreams did he have last night? Duck's brothers and sisters, Peace, Granola, Crystal, Chi, Aura, Tahini and the twins Yin and Yang, were always careening through the house like a litter of blond puppies yelping, "I'm not delirious, I'm in love."

Duck was the only one who never talked about his crushes since his crushes were on boys and Duck knew Darlene wouldn't understand at all. He thought it was strange because of how free she was about other things. Once she tried some pot brownies that Peace made but she said they just made her depressed and unable to stop giggling. She let Crystal's boyfriend sleep over and she had told all the girls that when they were ready to have sex she would take them for birth control. But when it came to Duck's secret he knew she wouldn't accept it. He had heard her talking to her best friend Honey-Marie about Honey-Marie's son Harley. Harley was a few years older than Duck, and Duck had always admired him from afar. He looked like he was born to play Prince Charming with his fistfuls of curly dark hair, flashing dark eyes and ballet dancer's body. He spoke in a soft rich voice and wore baggy cotton trousers with Birkenstocks and colorful socks. Harley was a waiter at a café in Santa Cruz but he really wanted to go to San Francisco and perform Shakespeare. Finally, just before he left, he told Honey-Marie that he was gay. She was devastated. Duck heard her tell his mother, "My heart is broken."

Then he heard his mother say, "It could be worse. He could have something really wrong with him."

He breathed a sigh of relief on the other side of the kitchen door.

"Something *is* wrong with him," Honey-Marie said.

Then Duck's mother said, "I guess you're right. I'd probably feel the same way if it was my own son."

After that Duck tried. He took Cherish Marine to the prom and bought her a huge corsage of pink lilies. He even rented a tux (although he would not put his feet in weasel shoes and wore his Vans instead). Cherish Marine was a bathing suit model and all the boys wanted to be her date but she liked Duck with his lilting surfer slur and teenage-Kewpie beauty. They danced all the slow dances and Duck felt Cherish Marine's bathing-suit-model-breasts pressing through her peach satin prom dress. They went to the pier with a group of other kids and shared a bottle of champagne which Cherish Marine liked to drink with a straw. They sat next to each other on the roller coaster, Cherish Marine's slender thigh pressing against Duck's leg, her hands grabbing his knee as their light bodies were thrown from side to side of the car, bruising, the metal bar hardly enough to keep them from being flung into space. But when the evening was over Duck walked Cherish to her door and kissed her good night on her smooth peachy cheek. She looked into his eyes waiting for something more but he only said, "You are a total babe. Thank you for being my date," and left.

Cherish Marine was stunned.

Duck went surfing because it was the only thing that comforted him. When he surfed he felt as aqua-blue and full and high as the waves but he also felt lost, a small human who could as easily be washed away as his father Eddie had been. Even the other surfers were separate from each other in their own tubes of water. Once in a while he'd see a guy holding his girlfriend and once he had seen a guy surfing with a pig on a leash. Duck wanted a boyfriend he could surf with, someone he could tell his secret to, someone who had the same secret inside. He wanted to reach inside his lover and touch that lonely secret with his own.

Duck decided to leave Santa Cruz. He drove his light-blue VW Bug along Highway 5 listening to the B-52s. He opened the windows and let the wind run its fingers through his shoulder-length hair that was bleached white from years of surfing in sun and salt water.

I am finally free, Duck thought, and then he thought about his brothers and sister and his mother telling them not to get sand all over everything and please be quiet so

I can do my yoga, Duck could you please pick up some tofu patties for dinner, you look just like your daddy I miss him so much he would have been so proud of you the way you rode that wave. The soaring free feeling was mixed with a sadness as Duck realized how alone he really was now. It was kind of like surfing—but then, Duck thought—everything was kind of like surfing.

Duck got to Zeroes at night and built a fire at the campground. He heated up a can of beans and watched the waves, nodding with encouragement at the good ones like a proud father, watching the sun drop into the sea. He thought of how his father had died in the ocean and how instead of hating the water or being afraid of it he loved it even more. He didn't understand why that had happened to his dad but now he knew that his dad's spirit was there in the waves protecting him. He wondered if his father would understand about how he loved boys. Somehow he thought that if his dad were alive his mom wouldn't have agreed with Honey-Marie. She would have been too happy basking in her love for Eddie Drake. Around Eddie Drake everyone just basked—they felt safe, they didn't judge. Duck had never heard his dad say a negative thing about anyone's personal choice—just about things like the Vietnam War and the assassination of Martin Luther King and what was happening to the oceans. Even now after his death, he was like the sun—falling into the waves, rising again every morning—still with Duck like a god in an ancient myth.

Duck slept on top of a picnic table that night with his arm around his surfboard. He looked up at the stars and wondered if the future love of his life was looking up at them too. He couldn't have known about the glow-in-the-dark stars on the ceiling of a room where a boy lay wishing for Duck.

Duck waxed his board and surfed-in the dawn; he felt as if he was pulling the sun up behind him as he rode the waves. Then he rinsed at the outdoor showers. He wanted to stay out by the water forever but he knew that if he was going to live in Los Angeles he would have to try to get work.

He applied at a surf shop in Santa Monica. He had worked at one in Santa Cruz and he knew a lot about boards. Plus there was something about Duck that made people like him right away—his grin and the innocent openness in his blue bay-window eyes. The owner of the shop told him he could start the next day.

When evening came Duck drove into town—to Santa Monica Boulevard. He had never seen so many gay men all at once. He felt the buzz of desire making them all beautiful. Everything was sexy here—hamburgers and ice cream and books and boots and even supermarkets became sexy. There was even a billboard advertising gay cruises. The men on the billboards were all tan and muscular and the men on the streets looked like they had stepped off the billboards. Music thumped out of bars, and through the doors Duck saw strobe lights pulsing. He wanted to dance. He had never danced with another man. Some men came out of a club with their hands in each other's back pockets. Sweat was pouring down their necks and arms. Someone whistled at Duck. He was afraid to look at who it was.

"Do you have some money for food?" a boy asked him. The boy had huge brown eyes. Duck gave him a couple of dollars even though he hadn't had dinner himself.

"Thanks, man," the boy said. He was different from some of the other guys around there—really young with a sweet mouth. When he smiled Duck saw that he had a gap between his front teeth. On the sidewalk in front of him was a huge chalk drawing of a beautiful blue angel.

"You new around here?" he asked.

Duck shrugged, not wanting to admit that this was his first time. His mouth felt dry and his heart was like the music coming out of the bars. "That's a good drawing," he said to change the subject.

"Thanks. Want to go to Rage?"

"Sure," Duck said.

The boy stood up and wiped his chalky hands on his jeans. Duck followed him into the bar that was crowded with men. A lot of the men knew the boy.

"Hey, Bam-Bam!"

"Is that you?" Duck asked.

The boy cocked his head. "Bam-Bam, yeah. Why?"

Duck started laughing. "My name is Duck," he said.

"Well at least it's not Pebbles."

Bam-Bam was a wild dancer, flinging his arms around and around over his head, gyrating his torso and hips. Duck found out later that sometimes he worked as a go-go boy when he could get a gig. Unfortunately it didn't pay much and most of the time Bam-Bam was out on the streets spare-changing or doing whatever else street kids did for some quick burger bucks.

"Where are you from?" Bam-Bam asked Duck over some beers that a guy in leather chaps had bought for them.

"Santa Cruz."

"And this is your first time out."

"What do you mean?"

"Out. Coming out."

"Oh. Yeah," said Duck. "I mean no."

"It's cool," Bam-Bam said. "Everyone has to have a first time."

"What about you?"

"I'm from all over. I was in Frisco last. I just keep moving. I'm a mover. I'm not from anywhere."

Duck nodded. He figured that wherever Bam-Bam was from—everyone had to come from somewhere, right?—it wasn't a two-story white frame house full of crystals and waffles and laughing golden children.

Maybe Bam-Bam really did come from nowhere. Duck had noticed some cigarette burn marks on Bam-Bam's bare, thin arms. Parents that did stuff like that to you had to become nothing nowhere in your head if you were going to make it out alive.

Duck and Bam-Bam went to the beach and slept on the picnic tables. In the morning Duck surfed while Bam-Bam sat on the sand and sketched him. Duck made them coffee, boiling water over the campfire.

"Do you like L.A.?" Duck asked.

"It's okay I guess. It'll be better when I get my shit together. I design furniture."

"Like what?"

"Well for now it's just drawings." Bam-Bam opened his sketch pad. He showed Duck pictures of tables made from surfboards and other ones covered with a mosaic of bottle caps and broken glass and china. There was some neo-Flintstone-style furniture made from broken slabs of stone and boulders, and some shaped like dinosaurs.

"You fully rip," Duck said.

Bam-Bam smiled so the gap between his teeth showed.

"So where do you live?" Duck finally asked.

"Sometimes I can find a squat. Sometimes I go to the shelter. When I have money I get a motel with some other kids. Why, you looking for a place?"

"Today I'm going to go look for an apartment," Duck said. "If you want you can stay with me for a while."

"How much?"

"It wouldn't cost you anything. And you could get off the streets."

Bam-Bam looked suspicious. Duck hoped he hadn't hurt his feelings. "I just don't know anybody out here," he added. "You could kind of show me around. You could design me a table. Just don't use my surfboard for a table!"

Duck and Bam-Bam found a one-bedroom apartment on Venice Beach. Duck surfed every morning and worked at the shop all day. At night he took an acting workshop but he was always too shy to present anything. After a while the teacher, Preston Delbert, just gave up and ignored Duck. But Duck kept going, sitting in the back, wondering if he would ever find a voice inside of him or something to say with it.

Bam-Bam stayed home painting murals of the ocean on the walls, designing furniture and making omelettes or peanut butter sandwiches for him and Duck to eat. He cut Duck's hair short so that it looked like the petals of a sunflower. Duck suggested that maybe Bam-Bam should take a class in furniture design at a city college or go to beauty school but Bam-Bam said he wasn't ready. He stopped going out altogether. He said he was afraid that he'd get caught back up in street life. At night, Duck and Bam-Bam slept in the same bed holding each other but they didn't make love. Bam-Bam said he didn't feel like it and Duck was too shy and inexperienced to push him. Duck wondered if he would ever know what it was like to make love to a boy he loved. Sometimes he wanted to go back to Rage or do something wild in a men's room or cruise in a park but he was afraid. He felt that he had to be responsible too, and set a good example for Bam-Bam.

One day Duck came back from work and saw that Bam-Bam's things were gone. There was a picture of an angel, like the chalk one on the sidewalk, painted above Duck's bed. Under it was written, "I love you, Duck. You will find your true angel. I am a dangerous one. Bam-Bam."

Duck sat on the bed and cried. He wasn't sure why he was crying so hard. I didn't know him that well, Duck told himself. He was a street kid. He couldn't stay inside with me forever. He wasn't my boyfriend, he didn't even want to make love with me. But still Duck cried. He was crying for the first person who knew his secret and for the painter of angels and for the warmth of those thin, cigarette-burned arms and maybe for something else—a premonition of what would happen later.

After Bam-Bam left, Duck went out every night, prowling the streets, maneuvering through them as if he was surfing perilous waves. He never talked to the men he touched in bathrooms and parks and cars. Is this what it means to be gay? Duck wondered. He missed the clean, quiet beaches of Santa Cruz, the softer sun and the sparkling, swirling colors of the waves and sky, the cathedral forests of redwood trees and the way he saw rabbits or long-legged baby deer who hopped like rabbits and heard the soft motorcycle hum of quail in the woods near his house. He missed being cleansed by the ocean he had practically grown up in, hiking home with his smiling sunlit dogs, sitting in the reeds by the pond listening to the frogs as evening slowly settled. He even missed the skinned-looking yellow slime banana slugs on the forest paths. Mostly, though, Duck missed his mother and his little brothers and sisters. He thought he could hear them squeal, "I'm not delirious, I'm in love!"—the words Duck felt he could never say. I guess I deserve this, Duck thought, holding a man in a cold-tiled, sour-smelling men's room. In the dark he could not even see the man's face and he was glad because he knew the man couldn't see him either.

Where are you? he called silently to his soul mate, the love of his life whose name he did not yet know. By the time I find you I may be so old and messed up you won't even recognize me. Maybe this is what I deserve for wanting to find a man. Looking for you always, never finding you, poisoning myself.

Then the lights from a passing car revealed the eyes

of the man whose hands were on Duck. The eyes were like tile. Duck shivered.

"Faggot," the man said. "How much do you hate yourself, faggot? Enough to come to piss stalls in the night? Enough to die?"

Duck tried to wrench away but the man had fingers in his arm like needles. He tried to scream but no sound came out of his throat to echo against the walls of the empty men's room.

"It is only a whisper now," the man hissed. "But it is coming. It is in your closest friend. Maybe it is in you, too."

That was when a light filled the doorway. In that radiance Duck was surprised to recognize something of himself. In that moment pulsing with a diffused rainbow mist of tenderness whispering, whispering, "Love comes, love comes," Duck was able to pull away and into the night. He felt as if he was surfing on a magic carpet and he thought he heard a voice calling to him, "Do you have a story to tell?"

When he got home Duck looked at his face in the mirror and saw that the bay windows in his eyes had clouded over and there was a roughness about his chin now. What story do I have to tell? Duck wondered.

The next night in his acting class Duck asked Preston Delbert if he could perform a monologue. Preston Delbert looked suspicious.

"I'd forgotten all about you, Duck," he said. "I don't think invisibility and muteness are very good traits for an actor."

"I know," said Duck. "But I have something to say now."

Duck got up in front of the class. His hands felt like they were covered with ice cream. He started to sit back down. Then he heard the voice asking if he had a story to tell. So Duck told the class the story of his mother and father and brothers and sisters. He told the story of Harley and Cherish Marine. And then Duck told the story of Bam-Bam. The class was silent. Some people had tears in their eyes. Duck felt as if his heart was an angel. Bam-Bam's sidewalk angel—that light, that full of light.

Soon Duck will meet his love. When Duck sees his love he will know that the rest of his story has begun. It will not be too late for either of them. The sweetness and openness they were born with will come back when they see each other in the swimming, surfing lights.

And we are still young, Duck will think. I wish I had met you when I was born, but we are still young pups.

They will still be young enough to do everything either of them has ever dreamed of doing, to feel everything they have always wanted to feel.

When they first kiss, there on the beach, they will kneel at the edge of the Pacific and say a prayer of thanks, sending all the stories of love inside them out in a fleet of bottles all across the oceans of the world.

And the story was over. Dirk felt he had lived it. Was it a story told to him by the man in the turban who now sat watching him from the foot of the bed? Had he dreamed it? Told it to himself? Whatever it was, it was already fading away leaving its warmth and tingle like the sun's rays after a day of surfing, still in the cells when evening comes.

"Who are you?" Dirk asked the man, his voice surfing over the waves of tears in his throat. "Who is Duck?"

"You know who I am, I think. You can call me by a lot of names. Stranger. Devil. Angel. Spirit. Guardian. You can call me Dirk. Genius if I do say so myself. Genie.

"Duck—you'll find out who he is someday."

"Why are you here?"

"Think about the word destroy," the man said. "Do you know what it is? De-story. Destroy. Destory. You see. And restore. That's re-story. Do you know that only two things have been proven to help survivors of the Holocaust? Massage is one. Telling their story is another. Being touched and touching. Telling your story is touching. It sets you free.

"You set some spirits free, Dirk," he went on. "You gave your story. And you have received the story that hasn't happened yet."

Dirk knew he had been given more than that. He was alive. He didn't hate himself now. There was love waiting; love would come.

He was aware, suddenly, of being in a dark tunnel, as if his body was the train full of fathers speeding through space toward a strange and glowing luminescence. He wanted that light more than he had wanted anything in his life. It was like Dirby, brilliant and bracing; it was a poem animating objects, animating his heart, pulling him toward it; it was a huge dazzling theater of love. On the stage that was that light he saw Gazelle in white crystal satin and lace chrysanthemums dancing with the genie, spinning round and round like folds of saltwater taffy. Dirk also saw the slim treelike form of a man in top hat and tails, surrounded with butterflies. When he looked more closely Dirk saw that they were not regular butterflies at all but butterfly wings attached to tiny naked girls who resembled young Fifis. Grandfather Derwood, Dirk thought. And Dirk saw Dirby too, Be-Bop Bo-Peep, tossing into the air wineglasses that became stars while Just Silver, balanced on the skull of death, held up her long ring-flashing hands and moved her head back and forth on her neck. He wanted to go to them. But there was one thing they were all saying to him over and over again.

"Not yet, not your time."

Dirk McDonald saw his Grandma Fifi sitting beside

him, her hair cotton-candy pink as the morning sun streamed in on it.

"Grandma," Dirk whispered. He looked around. White walls. The smell of disinfectant. Liquids dripping in tubes, into him.

"Where are we?"

"The hospital," Fifi said. "How do you feel?"

"Better."

"The doctor says you're going to be just fine."

"How long have you been here?"

"Oh, quite some time now. We've been telling each other stories, you and I, Baby Be-Bop. Past present future. Body mind soul," and Grandma Fifi squeezed Dirk's hand, knowing everything, loving him anyway.

Dirk closed his eyes. There was no tunnel but there was light—a sunflower-haired boy riding on waves the ever-changing colors of his irises.

Stories are like genies, Dirk thought. They can carry us into and through our sorrows. Sometimes they burn, sometimes they dance, sometimes they weep, sometimes they sing. Like genies, everyone has one. Like genies, sometimes we forget that we do.

Our stories can set us free, Dirk thought. When we set them free.